PRAISE FOR REBECCA LIM

'*The Astrologer's Daughter* is compulsively readable.
Avicenna is a captivating hero—tough yet vulnerable.
This gritty and mysterious love story will stay with
me for a long time.' Cath Crowley

'Smart and original—a beautifully written mash-up
of mystery, thriller and love story.' Vikki Wakefield

'[Lim's] taut, assured thriller weaves together astrology
and mythology, poetry and poverty…Teen and adult
readers who like their mysteries gritty and literary, with a
touch of magic: seek this one out.' *Kirkus Reviews* (Starred)

'A perfect balance of wit, humour, willpower
and raw emotion.' *Dolly*

'The best aspect of this novel was Avicenna herself…
a captivating combination of brazen and terrified.'
Launceston Examiner

'Subtly beautiful and utterly intriguing, Rebecca Lim's
Mercy series brims with mystery and romance that
pulls readers through the veil between worlds real and
mythical.' Andrea Cremer, *New York Times*-bestselling
author of *The Nightshade Series*

'Gripping. By the end, you can't help but wonder who this
angel of Mercy will become next.' *Sunday Herald Sun*

'What is compelling about this novel is not only its tightly
constructed plot but the lyrical quality of the writing…
Not to be missed.' *Reading Time*

Rebecca Lim is a writer and illustrator based in Melbourne, Australia. She worked as a commercial lawyer for several years before leaving to write full time. Rebecca is the author of sixteen books for children and young adult readers, including *The Astrologer's Daughter*. An Aurealis Awards finalist, Rebecca's work has been longlisted for the Davitt Award for YA, the Gold Inky Award and the CBCA Book of the Year Award for Older Readers. Her novels have been translated into German, French, Turkish, Portuguese and Polish.

afterlight

Rebecca Lim

(t)

TEXT PUBLISHING MELBOURNE AUSTRALIA

textpublishing.com.au

The Text Publishing Company
Swann House
22 William Street
Melbourne Victoria 3000
Australia

First published in 2015 by The Text Publishing Company

Cover and page design by Imogen Stubbs
Cover photographs: hand © Lia & Fahad / Stocksy United,
face © Maja Topčagić / Stocksy United
Typeset by J&M Typesetting

Printed in Australia by Griffin Press, an Accredited ISO AS/NZS 14001:2004 Environmental Management System printer

National Library of Australia Cataloguing-in-Publication entry:
Author: Lim, Rebecca (Rebecca Pec Ca), 1972-
Title: Afterlight / by Rebecca Lim.
ISBN: 9781925240498 (paperback)
ISBN: 9781922253255 (ebook)
Dewey Number: A823.4

This book is printed on paper certified against the Forest Stewardship Council® Standards. Griffin Press holds FSC chain-of-custody certification SGS-COC-005088. FSC promotes environmentally responsible, socially beneficial and economically viable management of the world's forests.

This project has been assisted by the Commonwealth Government through the Australia Council, its arts funding and advisory body.

To the people in my lifeboat:
Michael, Oscar, Leni and Yve.

With love always.

AFTERLIGHT

I have been one acquainted with the night.
I have walked out in rain—and back in rain.
I have outwalked the furthest city light.

ROBERT FROST (1928)

1

I used to believe in ghosts.

I saw something, once. It's not anything I've ever shared with anyone. I was little and he was real and it was dark and he only stood over me that one time when I was, maybe, five?

A tall man with a mass of long, pale hair, tied into a ragged plait. Sinewy and broad-shouldered, wearing a plaid shirt, jeans and boots. Heavy chains of silver at his throat and on his wrists. I could see all that, even with the light out.

But he was *real*. Real as you. And I was terrified. But all he did was look down at me, lying with my blankets pulled right up to my eyes, looking back up at him.

Then I breathed in—just a trembly, choky flutter, the tiniest sound—and he was gone.

But I don't believe, not anymore. Because if ghosts were real, Mum and Dad would have found a way—some way—to make it back to me. They promised me they'd always be there. There wasn't a day when they didn't say they loved me and we'd grow old together and they'd be there to look after all my babies while I took on the world, because the world was my oyster, I could be anything and do anything, I was better than them—which, based on my track record with boys and school, was never going to happen.

But they were optimists. It used to disgust me how much they looked on the bright side of life because before I came along, they said, life had never been bright. It had been hopeless. But I'd saved them. That was the word Mum had used: *Saved*.

They'd been through the wars, Dad used to remark. *Which means that me and your Mum are gonna live forever, Sophie. You'll never be rid of us.*

So when they were T-boned on the way up to Gippsland on Dad's Harley—taken out by an off-his-face random driving a stolen car—I expected…something. A miracle. At least a sign. Just a *Yoo hoo, love, we're okay.*

But there was no sign. Just a couple of matching white coffins a few days later, and a wake at my Grandma's pub that lasted for three days. Big bruisers in tatts and leather and Cuban-heeled boots from all over the country with names like Flasher and Fat Arse coming up to me all beery-breathed and teary-eyed, putting their meaty hands on my shoulders and giving them a squeeze, saying, 'Brother-in-arms, good man, the best.'

They were, though—the best dad and mum in the world, Joss and Angel. More like a couple of daggy, embarrassing friends than parents. No expectations, no bullshit; all love. And then, just like that—because of an old-times-sake Sunday motor up to the Lakes for a feel of the wind in their hair—the world no longer contained them.

◆

Around here, we've always been *those Teagues who live down the pub*.

So after Dad and Mum died, I just kept on living at Gran's place—The Star Hotel—the way I've always lived there. Life involved the same bedroom, the same clothes, the same school and the same pervasive smell of beer. Only, someone had taken a God-sized eraser to part of it. They were taken from me in the November before my final year was due to kick off. They died before I'd finally be old enough to vote or drink. It felt like the cruellest, most irreversible joke.

It also felt unreal for the first few months. Like I'd open the storeroom door and Dad might be standing there with his back to me, stacking bulk lots of toilet rolls. Or I'd take out the garbage and somehow catch Mum sneaking a cigarette in the laneway behind the pub.

It made me a little crazy. I'd sit for hours inside the built-in wardrobe in their bedroom, just so that the air would smell of them. I'd talk to complete strangers at random hoping they'd ask me how I was and then spring my tragic story on them only to watch those same people run away in horror. I cried in public places and walked the streets around The Star after dark, practically begging to be murdered because the dark was *where they were*; they were nowhere in the light.

For a while, I convinced myself they were just on the round-the-world cruise Mum had always wanted to go on—only they'd forgotten to send me postcards. And craziest of all? I walked up to Floyd Parker the first week that school was back and kissed him on the mouth in front of actual witnesses, for seconds that felt like hours. I had a death wish, obviously. Life was short, it had been proven, and if I never did it, I'd never do it. Now, now was the time. There was nothing left to lose.

Stick legs and hair, that's what I was known for. Hair like that *L'Oreal* bird, the old one, not Beyoncé or Eva or Doutzen. A curly, ginger cloud, so thick and crazy it looked too big for my head. And freckles—I only had to step out into the light for a new infestation to start somewhere. I was already 183.5 centimetres without shoes on and in possession of hair-trigger blood vessels in the face. No meat on me to speak of. All bones and angles.

So I deserved the ensuing hilarity. Floyd Parker had lived across the road, six doors down, for years and years. We'd even walked in to school together; I couldn't count how many times. But he'd never shown me anything other than benevolent disinterest, a fact I recklessly disregarded when I pulled him to me. He was hot—only growing hotter—and I was a mess. What I'd done was completely mental. Like a lemming, I'd thrown myself at him and he'd side-stepped and let me go over the cliff.

'The way he recoiled, Soph,' someone hooted later, 'was a classic.'

Just like with death, you can never go back after something like that. In the panicky days after, when I started skipping class and stopped taking the calls of anyone I ever knew from my old life—I somehow convinced Gran to let me change schools just so I'd never have to look Floyd Parker in the eye again.

It's the start of final year, I'd begged. *You don't want me to stuff it up any more than it's already been stuffed, do you?*

I'd been watching the evening news with Gran when

I broached the subject—the lead story about some terrible shooting that had taken place that day at a city intersection. Some outlaw motorcycle gang leader with a neck almost as wide as his shoulders had shot an innocent bystander to death when he intervened in a domestic the psycho was having with his on-off girlfriend. A backpacker got hurt, too, plus a woman who was in a car at the lights. The bikie was still on the run. It was unclear what had happened to the girlfriend.

Her photo had lingered for a moment on screen. 'She looks just like your mother,' Gran had whispered, her fork frozen halfway to her mouth. 'Same long, dark hair, pale skin; beautiful. Could *be* your mother. It's uncanny. And the gunman was a Reaver, just like your dad was once. The great untouchable *O'Loughlin* himself. Haven't heard that name in years. What are the chances?'

I'd registered the coincidences dully. The girl in the mug shot—staring up and out of her long hair, wary, like something cornered—looked more my age than Mum's. But they could have been sisters, yeah. And the fact that a bikie and a dancer were involved was eerie.

'Like history repeating itself,' I'd mumbled, swallowing. 'Only Dad was no psycho, Gran. He got Mum *out* of the business the same way he got himself out. And I never heard them argue. Not once. He would sooner have turned a gun on himself, than on Mum. She was his *life*.'

Seconds later, I'd placed my fork down on the plate balanced on my lap overwhelmed by sorrow: Mum, Dad, *Floyd*. Nothing left to live for. 'I am *destroyed*,' I whispered, head in my hands, the tears dripping down into the mash, the untouched bean salsa.

'A fresh start, Sophie,' Gran had agreed finally—freaked out just as much by my behaviour as by the news story, but trying not to show it as she got up to take our plates back to the kitchen before the night shift began—'might be just what you need.'

✦

So I found myself at Ivy Street High two Mondays later. It was just a twenty-minute walk from my old school, a simple detour, nothing really, but it could have been a different country I was crossing into because no one knew my story.

They'd all just stared and stared at me going up and up and up when I'd walked in the gates on my first day. A freak who blocked out the sun. Tallest girl there by miles.

'Sure you don't want the technical institute, Storkie?' a guy had drawled as I fetched up at the door of the special common room for final year students. I'd stood there looking lopsided in my second-hand, bile-yellow and navy uniform, ginger hair as fat as a fox tail hanging over one shoulder, trying to gauge the tribal connections, too green to see the pattern of how they all fitted in.

And I'd done that thing I *hate* about myself, which involves most of the blood in my body making a sudden leap for my neck, then my face, then my scalp, like a live thing running for cover in my hair. *Blushing* doesn't even begin to describe what happens when I get embarrassed. Everyone had laughed while I'd kicked at the carpet, my face on flaming *fire*, and that was how it was from then on. Open season on tall jokes.

But I'd survived my first day, talking to nobody, smiling gamely into the middle distance, assiduously avoiding the three girls people kept pointing out to me as *the toughest bitches at Ivy Street*. It was enough, I told myself over and over, that I'd never have to walk past Floyd Parker's house again. I could do this. Nine months more and even school would be a distant memory. I wasn't dumb, exactly. But school and I had just never rubbed along. We'd just never *gotten* each other and I was glad to be just about out the back end of it.

After that first day, *Storkie* stuck. It didn't matter that I was Sophie Teague any more, the girl with the two dead parents. At Ivy Street High, I was a clean skin. New game; new rules. Play on.

Then, as I was lying in bed that very night, listening

8

to public radio in the dark—someone's idea of a dirty garage, Ramones tribute band—the room suddenly began to smell of some old-fashioned flowery perfume and *she* was bending over me like I was a sick person in need of assistance.

The girl from the news. The missing stripper.

In my bedroom.

And I was five years old again, in the dark. Heart stopped, everything stopped.

She'd looked real and solid and solemn. A girl with a pale, unlined face who could have been my dead mother's daughter she looked so much like her. I could tell all this, because the girl was outlined in a faint silvery light. Her hair was slightly wavy at the ends and she had a strong nose. Her lower lip was a little fuller than her upper one, and she was of just above average height. I could also see how, if she didn't watch it, she'd run to fat one day with no problems. But that right now, she was shaped like an extra busty hourglass—something guys like that I knew I would *never* be.

She wore a black tank top and black jeans, long hair hanging down loose, eyes like pieces of jet, long feet pale and bare. Beautiful, in a top-heavy, fleshy kind of way. Silent, just looking at me looking at her. Kind of illuminated from the inside, and in outline, like a freaking *torch*.

It felt like I was wide-awake in the dark for hours,

literally suspended in place by terror. While for her, it probably felt like no time had passed at all. It was hard to get a handle on what she was thinking because her face never changed the whole time.

It was probably more of a reconnaissance manoeuvre, a scouting exercise, on her part. If I'd leapt out of bed and turned on all the lights, screamed at her to leave, or made the sign of the cross, hissed, spat, done anything, maybe she would've gone away and stayed away.

No prizes for guessing who just lay there, too scared even to blink, while she studied me like a painting for surface weaknesses, for flaws. She probably took one look at me and thought to herself, *There's my bitch*. And that's how it started.

2

So she came again, the next night, and the next, until I got what she wanted.

Eve. That was what I ended up calling her—I had to call her something, and she was sort of a bit biblical looking, and a bit evil, all at the same time.

Anyway, on the Tuesday afternoon, I'd been stacking trays of empties into the industrial dishwasher just to escape our resident pervert, Dirty Neil, who treated Gran's Public Bar like it was his lounge room. He was long-term unemployed and had to be at least thirty-five—looking more like fifty-five because of all the beer and Bacardi he drank.

Watched you grow up, he said, like he always did as he

took up position on his favourite bar stool, licking his lips while he said it. I hadn't yet worked out what was creepier—the thought of him thinking he was good enough for me, or the thought of him thinking *about* me.

So I'd avoided going near him, or up to my bedroom, for hours. Instead, I'd surrounded myself with kitchen hands, noises, *things*. But every third Tuesday it was The Star's infamous $10 Scotch Fillet and Pub Bingo Night, which brought out every tight-arse punter in the galaxy. When the bingo was on and the steaks were chargrilling, an entire hostile intergalactic force could land on the roof and come through shooting, and no one would be the wiser. While The Star heaved beneath me to its usual bingo night rhythms, I convinced myself that it was safe to go back upstairs and that Eve wouldn't be back; Monday night had to be a one-off. If I slept with all the lights on, I reasoned with myself, I'd be okay.

But you don't really have a hope of blocking out someone who can walk through a deadlocked door. I smelt the perfume first, and then I knew. Turned to face her, drenched in an icy sweat, nearly screaming the house down, until I remembered that at our place no one can hear you scream—and even if they did, they'd just put their head down and keep drinking, so there was no point.

11.18pm. That's what the clock radio said. I had the

edge of my doona gripped tight in my hand, about to climb in and get cosy.

But I froze instead—with her staring at me staring at her. It was a Mexican freaking stand-off between me and a walking dream, with only the length of the bed between us.

This time, she had a message for me.

In pictures, not words, because Eve doesn't talk, exactly. She doesn't have a voice like we do. It's more that she just looked at you and you'd *know* what she wanted because she'd put it straight into your head.

But on that day—the Tuesday—I didn't understand and refused to look at her while she showed me:

> *A school.*
> *A school kid.*
> *A car.*

In reply, I simply fumbled my clock radio on and turned it up to maximum volume. Followed that by jumping into bed and pulling the covers right over my head to block out *her*, the light, the smell. So scared that I said nothing and did nothing and eventually, hours later, eons later, one endless silent scream later, she left, taking the smell of flowers with her.

The third night—the Wednesday—Gran even came in while Eve was actually standing there giving me her unblinking, death-ray stare. All the lights were on, the music, even the fan because it'd been right by my bed and I'd run out of ideas. Everything was full-blast. I dunno, I think I was trying to *blow* Eve away. Obviously, it wasn't working. Nothing about her moved. Nothing about *me* moved. Stalemate.

But then Gran burst through the door and practically stood on top of Eve, demanding to know why I'd quit helping Cook early *when we're already two down tonight and really struggling, Soph, how selfish are you?* She was too cross to see how terrified I was, that I hadn't moved out of the position I'd been lying in for so long there was almost no blood left in my brain.

I unfroze long enough to ask Gran in a funny little voice if she could *smell* anything.

All *I* could smell was that old-fashioned, talcum-powdery smell that Eve always brought with her like a choking cloud. I hated perfume anyway, and I was coming to hate this one like *the toughest bitches at Ivy Street* hated some poor kid called Linda Jelly.

If it was possible, Gran looked even madder after I said that and waved her arms right *through* Eve. Who, to my eyes, looked as solid as the next person. It was only the way the light hit her that was the faintest bit *wrong*.

'All I can smell,' Gran shouted, 'is bloody lemongrass-infused pot roast! Told Cook we wouldn't be able to shift the stuff, but never mind *me*. I just own the place! Now stop listening to that headbanging shit, Soph! We can hear it through the goddamn *floor*. Either you get your backside downstairs to help out or you *go to sleep*.'

She stormed off before I could begin to croak: *Help me, please*.

So Gran couldn't *see* Eve or *smell* her. Meanwhile, Eve hadn't once taken her eyes off me, not through any of it. She just continued to stand at the foot of my bed, hands lightly curled at her sides, dark gaze unwavering. She didn't bother to tell me again what she wanted, so while I lay there, feeling fainter and fainter, I finally forced my sluggish brain to really think about what she'd, uh, *told* me so far.

A school. Somewhere.

On a main road. Lots of kids. Little kids.

Something to do with a little blond boy in a navy cap, a light-blue sweatshirt, navy shorts, white runners and socks.

A red car.

Great.

Having Gran go off in my face like a firecracker actually helped, in a weird kind of way, because for the first time I actually *spoke* to Eve. Both of my hands had fallen asleep and I knew I had to do something. This couldn't go on. I would probably die here before I understood what she wanted.

'Um, I don't understand,' I said. Well, more like barely whispered. 'And I'd really like to go to bed now, if that's all right with you. But thanks for, uh, visiting.'

I waited tensely, only breathing again when Eve didn't turn into a shrieking gorgon with a rotating head. Her expression didn't even change. She didn't cause my walls to weep blood or the curtains to catch on fire or the souls of ten thousand dead people to rise up through the floorboards and surround me. She just kept on looking. And waiting.

I flexed a knee experimentally and the sky didn't fall in, so I rolled over slowly and sat up, facing her.

'*I'm. Sorry. I. Don't. Understand*,' I said. A little louder and slower this time, as if Eve were deaf and stupid. I guess I was getting braver.

Then she suddenly pushed the same handful of images at me again. It was like I was seeing something that was streaming at the wrong speed. And you can't tell someone like Eve to *slow down* or *rewind* or *zoom out*. It just doesn't work like that.

School, kid, red car. Over and over, until other details began to fly out at me that I hadn't seen because I'd been too freaked-out to concentrate properly.

What school? A primary school. *Wattle Valley Primary*. See that sign behind the little kid's head? That's what it said.

What time of day was it? Home time. See how everyone was leaving and getting into cars and driving away?

The kid? Piece of piss. He was walking home. *Somebody give me a medal.*

The car had me stumped, though. It was an early-model red Ford, with rusting paintwork. More of a bomb really, with a dog in the back, a kelpie. Couldn't see who was driving. Couldn't see the number plate. Could've meant anything. Someone's dad, someone's mum, more info please.

Finally, I shook my head at Eve and told her to stop. *Stop.*

And it did, like she'd opened a window in my head to let the breeze in and the pictures out.

I shrugged apologetically, hoping she'd take the hint and take a hike. 'Still don't get it,' I said. 'You'll have to find someone else to tell your little story to, sorry. See ya.'

It was pretty weird, but I was almost comfortable with Eve by this stage. I mean, we were practically conversing. So I wasn't expecting what happened next.

Now, the whole time she hadn't moved a muscle. Not a hair. But when I told her to *go*, when she thought I wasn't going to *try* any more, that comfortable feeling vanished like an arctic gale descending because she just pushed the whole show reel—*school, kid, red car*—at me with the force and speed of a sonic boom and I blacked out.

When I came to, with a feeling like somebody was dancing on my grave, she was gone. But I'd finally got it. Those things she'd tried to burn into my brain? She wanted me to *go* there. She wanted me to figure it out. She wanted me to *see* what she'd shown me with my own eyes.

◆

That night, I don't think I slept. I kept thinking about Dad and Mum and how they always believed in stupid, hokey sayings like *Third time's a charm*.

In my case, it wasn't a charm. It was a sign. The one I'd been begging for; that said that maybe they were all right—wherever they were—and they wanted me to know that.

Eve was the message. She had to be.

Because this nameless creature—the spit of my mum—shows up in my bedroom, right? *Three times*. Two weeks, roughly, after I'd first caught her face on the telly and four months, almost, to the day Mum and Dad vanished into the great hereafter on the spirit of Dad's Harley.

Maybe they sent Eve because they couldn't come themselves and she needed help. Dad had helped plenty of people over the years. Mates who'd lost everything would often drop in for a night that turned into weeks. Old men without money or family would often get a free shout, to Gran's great annoyance.

Something bad had happened to Eve; that much was plain. The fact Eve had found me—*me*, and not someone else—had to mean something. If I'd been in her position I would've wanted me to help. I was a soft touch; Mum always said so. Strangers came up and talked to me all the time; I had that kind of face. I couldn't count how many fallen little old ladies I'd had to help up at my local shopping centre over the years. Mum used to shake her head when I told her about the two homeless kids who always took money off me at the bus stop near the pub. 'You're as bad as your father,' she'd say. 'Both of you, *marsh-mallows*. But'—and her eyes would get this suspicious shine whenever she told me this —'any creature comes to you for help, you bloody *help* them because I was that creature, once…'

She never usually finished that sentence.

If Eve knew I was a soft touch, well, someone who knew me on the other side had to have primed her with the info, I reasoned.

For them, I would do it for them. Find the school, the kid, the car.

❖

The next day, I almost had a false start. Thinking about it now makes my blood run cold because anything could've happened. There were two Wattle Valley Primary Schools in the directory and I just picked the closest one because I was lazy and half convinced I'd dreamt the whole thing up.

Anyway, it being very much apparent that no hot guy in his right mind was going to ask me out that Thursday afternoon, or any afternoon for that matter, I stopped in at the pub and begged a couple of hours off after my double spare. Gran grudgingly agreed. Dirty Neil was disappointed when I mooched back out the door at 2.06pm, but I was sick of trying to dodge him as I did the general mop up and heartily sick of providing eye candy for perverts at no extra charge. And did I tell you that The Star Hotel specialises in male patrons who can't aim straight? Doing Eve's dirty work had to be a step up from all of that.

I caught a tram that ran through the city, then hopped on another that ran out to the bayside suburb that hosted the Wattle Valley Primary I'd decided to stake out.

It felt like it was about ten degrees outside, so you can imagine my gratitude when I got there. It was 3.17 by the time I took up my position under an extensively shat-upon tree, and at precisely 3.23 the front doors exploded outwards as little kids of every size and description flooded onto the pavement in front of me, all in identical navy caps, navy shorts and powder-blue sweatshirts. Finding a little kid who looked like the blond kid in Eve's—and I say that loosely—*instructions* would be a big ask, I thought, as I started scanning every face that came through the gates. Figuring out what to do with him once I found him, though, would be even harder. What was I even *doing* here?

In the end, it wasn't me that found him; it was the driver of the red car. I'd totally forgotten about it. Some detective I'd make. By 3.32, I was angry with myself, furious at Eve, and ready to throw in the towel and head home when I saw a red car do a slow U-turn through a sea of double-parked cars and start wobbling up the street away from me. It stood out a mile among the shiny 4WDs and late-model family wagons. In case it was important, I wrote the number plate down on the back of my hand with a felt tip I had in my pocket. Scared enough of pissing Eve off that I wanted to get it right first go, so that I could report back properly later. Not that I was sure she'd be listening. Or that she'd even be there to tell.

So the car wasn't hard to spot, was it? And about five minutes later, I saw this boy up ahead, getting smaller all the time. He was tiny anyway, and he had his head down, and he was walking, and it made my skin come out in goosebumps because it was *the kid*, the one Eve had burned into the back of my eyes. Not sure if I should approach him directly, I followed him and the car for two more blocks, at a distance, until they both turned into a side street and I lost sight of them. I began to run, skidding as I rounded the corner and saw the boy leaning against the front passenger door of the red car, talking to the men inside. He was smiling and nodding, the dog hanging out the back window, all friendly. Suddenly, there was his little hand on the door, his school bag already inside. And my first thought was: *What does Eve want me to do now?*

Now, I've never claimed to possess any sixth sense, or second sight. But, oh boy, did I know a pervert when I saw one. They came into our place all the time—hey, we even had one of our own practically living-in—so I knew, without having to examine the feeling very closely, that it was really important to keep the little kid out of the car. He just *couldn't* get in.

So I shouted, 'Oi! Oi, *you*, kid!'

And the kid turned, his leg already halfway through the open back door, the dog pushing its snout back out at the noise, baring its teeth, ready to give it to me. I frantically fished for something to say next, the two men in front simultaneously shooting me murderous greasies and urging the boy to get in, get in quickly, shut the door, there's no time to waste. The boy turned back, his head already in, then his shoulders. He didn't know me and he trusted them. What did they *say* to him? They had a dog. I *had* to get his attention.

'Kid! Kid! You dropped something back there!' I screamed, pointing over my shoulder. 'If you lose it, your mum's going to kill you!'

That made the boy hesitate. She-who-must-be-obeyed loomed large in everyone's life, especially a little kid's. He was so small he'd probably only just stopped wetting his bed and still had his dinner cut up for him at night.

The boy stepped back and turned towards me again, and that's when I yelled out, 'You're gone! You're history! We're onto you!' to the two pervs in the red car, and they gunned it out of there, the kid's bag still inside, the door swinging open, the dog doing 360s in the back seat, as they turned the corner on two wheels, practically. The boy flew backwards on his bum onto the road and burst into tears.

It had all happened so *fast*.

The little guy cried all the way home and wouldn't hold my hand properly the entire time, because I'd lied and the nice men still had his schoolbag and his mum *really* was going to kill him now. Only she didn't, because once she got home and I explained why I was sitting on her front doorstep with her weeping, angry child, she cried too, and gripped my fingers so hard in gratitude they almost fell off.

While the kid watched afternoon TV with a plate of choc-olate biscuits piled high in front of him, we even rang

Crime Stoppers together with the details I'd written on the back of my hand. Then she made me a cup of tea I couldn't drink because my pounding heart was still lodged somewhere in my throat.

As I jumped back on the tram afterwards, I found myself thinking I couldn't wait to tell Eve what had happened, which is as twisted as it sounds.

3

When Eve didn't return that night, I thought she was gone for good and chalked it down to a restless spirit with one more good deed to do before she departed for the ever after. The thing, I reasoned, was done and dusted. And it felt good, that I'd been able to help.

How wrong was I?

Two nights later, when the pub was finally quiet (if you ignored the jukebox machine on the landing doing its flashy, sorting, *winky winky* thing every half hour, and the occasional noises the building made that sometimes sounded like random gunshot), Eve came again.

I was a heavy sleeper once I got going—you'd need to drive a prime mover through my bedroom to wake me once I was sound asleep—but, suddenly, I was completely and totally in the present and she was bending over me again, in the pitch dark of my upstairs bedroom, outlined faintly in silver. Her long hair hanging loose and smooth. All in black as usual, bare arms, bare feet. Eerie-beautiful.

'Hi,' I said, sitting up and edging away from her, remembering what she was capable of, my knees drawn up under my chin for extra protection. 'You were right, the kid needed your, my, uh, *our* help. He's got no dad—ran off with his PA last year. Mum works two jobs and can't drive him. They're going to be a lot more careful next time.'

Eve straightened, shimmering beside the bed in her usual get up, her face all straight lines. No joy, no anger, no sorrow. Just business.

As though she'd said it, I thought: *Next*.

And she'd laid it all in front of me like a map—in pictures, not words, because like I said, she doesn't speak like we do because she's got nothing to speak *with*, has she?

I didn't need to close my eyes to see a T-intersection, a white-haired white guy in a dark-blue blazer, gold buttons, white shirt, beige trousers, grey loafers. About to step out in front of a speeding car. A black ute, tricked up with mirror-image naked girl decals, in disco-ball silver, on the back window. For good measure, Eve showed me the same thing, five times. It was like a *Visions for Beginners* tutorial, but on her terms, and hers alone.

Like it was projected across the walls, I saw:

Kemal's Kebab Shop, 100% Halal, on one corner, a charcoal chicken shop, *Henny Penny* on the other.

Across the street, two banks, a KFC, and a TAB. Colours dull in the daylight. Piece of cake. Clear as crystal. Sorted.

'It's not going to stop, is it?' I said out loud. She didn't need to nod because she's got a better trick than that. She just vanished.

✦

As soon as I fell out of bed the next morning, I called Eric, the twenty-eight-year-old part-time DJ, part-time uni student, dreadlocked dish pig, and told him to swap Sunday kitchen duties with me. Even knowing what I was in for when I returned to The Star didn't dampen my enthusiasm.

Someone needed help. I could almost hear triumphal music as I boarded the tram, bending to get under the dangling fluorescent green handholds while negotiating the mohair-wearing uni students who smelt of bong smoke, the seniors with faces like cats' bums, the God-awful smell of years of trapped BO in the air.

Storkie's come to save the day! my inner voice sang. It felt good, doing something. It took my mind off the panicky feeling of loss that followed me every moment I was awake. I would be their daughter and do this thing, and maybe that feeling would one day recede.

Only, when I got to the pedestrian crossing in front of Kemal's Kebab Shop, there was no one there. In my excitement I hadn't registered what time of day the man in the suit jacket would arrive. Daytime sure, but morning? Afternoon? While the sun was still in the sky, he could come any time.

It was 10.43am and nothing was happening at that icy intersection except two people stumbling into the KFC for a Sunday morning grease fix. An all-day stake out was *not* an option. Not with Eric due to clock off at 12pm and Gran liable to blow a gasket if I failed to show. I loved Gran, don't get me wrong, and she loved me back with all her heart, but she wasn't the most even-tempered lady.

I heard him before I saw him. At least, I heard the ripples that follow everywhere in his wake because he was the type of guy, I learned later, that can't resist calling a passing Vietnamese girl a *chink* or telling a North African taxi driver to go home, *if you know how to get there, you dirty kaffir*. He was a prick, and this was one of the biggest immigrant suburbs in the inner city, so it was a spark and tinder situation. But I didn't know that when I was loitering with intent outside Kemal's Kebabery. All I knew was that an old guy in old guy clothes that matched Eve's description exactly was coming my way and I had to save him.

Problem was: where was the car? There was nothing to save him *from*. I scanned the T-intersection quickly as the old man strode towards the pedestrian crossing, talking to himself and looking red in the face, like he was about to have a giant heart attack right there on the spot. Maybe Eve had been wrong. Maybe it wasn't going to be a car. Maybe he was destined to drop dead at my size 11 feet. I didn't fancy giving this guy mouth-to-mouth *at all*.

Please, please, I thought to myself as he came up beside me. *Please let it* not *be* that.

He punched the button five times quickly, like that would make the lights change any faster, while I twitched around nervily on the spot and debated what to do. Behind us, someone leant out of Kemal's and shouted something to the effect of 'Hey, fuckhead!' while the man beside me swung around pretty niftily for an old fart and gave him a big, visual *fuck you* right back. Nice.

The lights changed. Still no car. But something told me I had to keep the old man from stepping off the kerb.

'You can't cross now,' I said desperately, moving to stand right in front of him. Meanwhile, the pedestrian light continued its demented pinging, about to click over to red.

Eve had been *wrong*. A red flush whooshed up my neck into my head, which I was pretty certain would soon blow off with embarrassment.

The old guy reared back, then muscled forward. 'You with them, you little slut?' He jerked his head at the shops behind us, moving in so close I could smell strong *eau de armpit* and something that reminded me of wet socks and braised cabbage all rolled up together and boiled some more. I had a bird's eye view of the dandruff that lay along his shoulders like a thick drift of snow.

'Just trust me,' I said, looking over the old man's pink and flaky bald patch for that bloody, bloody car, which existed nowhere at present except inside my head. 'You don't want to do that.'

Maybe it wasn't supposed to be today. Maybe I had to go home and come back tomorrow and hope he'd be *right here* for me to accost again. I punched the pedestrian crossing button on autopilot. Old sewer-breath didn't bother to reply. I thought we were safe.

When the lights changed for a second time, I was still facing his way, with my back to the crossing. Without warning, the man whose life I supposedly held in my hands just shoved me into the street so hard I almost fell on my bony arse.

As I struggled to keep from going down on the wet bitumen, I saw it, I saw *the car*, about to run a red into the

T and mow the old bastard down. He was halfway across, so busy still mouthing off at me over his shoulder that he didn't see death coming for him with matching naked-girl decals gleaming in the thin sunshine.

You won't catch me saying this most of the time, but sometimes being a freak *can* be useful, an unexpected gift. All that Goal Defence I'd been forced to do all my life was finally good for something. I don't remember doing it, but people say I pulled off a feat no one should have been able to pull off that quickly. It was split second stuff. The guy was already too far ahead. It was already too late. They said it was superhuman.

They also say that I broke his nose, but based on what I found out about him later—how much everyone on the street feared and detested him—he deserved that much.

It made the evening news, the next day's papers. All the locals they interviewed said it was a nice thing I did, but I should have let him die.

4

The slow clapping and foot stomping began when I entered our form room on Monday morning. Most faces were friendly or coolly indifferent, which was fine by me. Simon Pandeli drawled, 'Nice work!' and Biddy Cole yelled out, 'Way to go, Stork. On ya.'

But some were openly hostile. Like Claudia P. and her posse of skinny-jeans wearing, Napoleon Perdis-abusing, ghd-wielding super clones; the very *bitches* I'd been told to avoid.

I could see that they couldn't believe how I'd gone from zero to hero overnight. I'd been everywhere—on TV, on talkback radio, all positive about *the youth of today*, for a change. They were calling me *inspirational* and *enigmatic*, *heaven sent*. That last one gave me a laugh; if only they knew.

A trio of comedians on a commercial radio station had even started a campaign to get me knighted, they'd written to the Queen and everything. A reporter for *Today Tonight* had doorstepped me before school when I was still wearing my nightgown and Uggs, my bad case of bed head a sculpture-unto-itself as I picked up the morning papers out the front of The Star. Now the whole country knew what I wore to bed and what I looked like after I got out of it, and I'd been trying to block that thought out of my mind ever since.

Today Tonight had taken matters into their own hands because I hadn't made myself 'available' to answer any questions. When the reporter had thrust the microphone under my nose and said urgently, 'So give us an insight into exactly how it was that you happened to be in the right place at the right time?' I'd muttered, 'Must be psychic, mate,' and shut the door in his face.

But I was like wallpaper. Like grass. No one at Ivy Street could ever remember a word I'd said after I said it. And any half-clever thing that came out of my mouth was invariably attributed to the person standing next to me. I was kind of invisible, which is as mad as it sounds.

Once, I'd overheard my maths teacher say: *If there's oxygen up where she is, none of us are breathing it.* But she would say that. We had a love-hate relationship, me and Mrs McKendry.

So by second period, what I'd been up to was so ancient history that everyone was hanging out for recess and news about the latest hook-ups, two-way, three-way, whatever. As usual, every girl who wasn't an out-and-out lesbo was waiting to get a look at Jordan Haig, the most seriously beautiful guy in Year 12 and so off limits that even Claudia P. and her chain-smoking fembots couldn't touch him. The way he gave people the brush-off was an art form and just one more thing to love about him.

I had one class with Jordan—Biology—but that wasn't enough to get me by, and like everyone else, I was waiting to eyeball him and his two closest mates as they did their aloof rebel thing in the corner of the quadrangle that made up the centre of the school universe. Darwinian stuff went on at Ivy Street High. Every day, there was at least someone punching on someone else, or getting their extended family involved so that Asian-Maori, Skippy-Greek, girl-on-girl all-ins were always erupting outside the school gates—knives, nunchuks and everything—soon as the bell went.

But even the die-hard jocks, the death-metal freaks, the tech-heads, the skateboarders, the self-starting entrepreneurs and the dorks-who-ran-in-packs-for-safety thought Jordan Haig was untouchably cool. No one except his two besties knew anything about him, and they never spilled their guts. There was a mystery at the core of him that everyone could see, but nobody could fathom.

He had dark hair, with eyes as grey as rain-washed skies, and he always dressed like a druggy rock star god, all jangly silver and onyx around his wrists and around his neck. Some days, he wore cut-off tees that highlighted his incredible tatts. One of his arms sported a full sleeve of crazy words and symbols, all intertwined and tricked out in blues, greens, reds and blacks. The other arm was only half-done, from wrist to elbow. But the guy could clearly stand *pain* and that was enough to make him object of lust and/or envy No. 1.

And he was tall, taller than me (Yes, there was a God), and when he chose to speak—which wasn't too often— they could never catch him out, the teachers, because he always knew the answer, even though he looked like a hood-on-the-make. He was whip-smart and nothing ever fazed him, which said heaps about Jordan Haig because when you're eighteen, awkwardness goes with the terrain, and he was never that.

So I saw him, finally, that morning I was almost notorious, huddled beside Biddy Cole and her marginally friendly BFFs. For me, the day had really only started, was only really bearable, because I'd seen him. As I stared over at Jordan, I wondered whether my being a household name might somehow make him aware I was even alive, until I reminded myself what had happened when *looking* turned to *touching* in the case of Floyd Parker and my face suddenly flamed up so red that Biddy asked me if I was choking on my apple.

But maybe all the coverage *had* helped because, weirdly, as I binned my morning tea—some horrible pub-menu experiment wrapped in filo pastry that had gone wrong— Jordan actually looked up as I passed him by, on my way to Art.

As our eyes met for the first time in recorded history, and I suddenly stopped remembering how to breathe, the blood drained out of *his* face.

Should be the other way around, I thought, startled. Then Jordan turned his back on me, quite deliberately, and walked away.

✦

A locked bathroom door usually signalled *trouble* and kept the punters away, just grateful it wasn't them inside, begging for mercy. But I was stupid, and I was busting, and just before the final class of the day I tried the door handle on the third floor girls' toilets once too often.

Sharys F.—Claudia P.'s chief goon—suddenly opened the door and yanked me inside, where I fell into a scene out of *Mean Girls* redux. Only, this being here and not

Hollywood, no one was good looking and everyone was dressed badly.

Turned out Claudia had her nemesis—Linda Jelly—in a chokehold, up against the wall of the last cubicle. Sharys frogmarched me right up to the action, making certain I couldn't look away. Linda Jelly, with her mild scoliosis, Coke-bottle glasses, dumpy figure and inexplicable chin-length perm, had always been an easy target, Biddy had once confided. 'I never join in the general Linda-bashing that goes on,' she'd chattered, pointing out the back of Linda's head over her open textbook, 'but I've never tried to defend her either, I'm sorry to say, because I like to pretend I'm *Switzerland*.'

Claudia didn't miss a beat—not acknowledging me exactly, but still somehow making me feel included. 'Got your period today, Jelly Belly?' she said conversationally as Sharys and Goon Two—a girl whose parents had named her after a musical term like *Cadence* or *Rhapsody*, I forgot what—crowded around to watch.

Even if Linda had been able to answer, she didn't have to. A huge patch of blood had leaked through the back of her school uniform and whenever Claudia gave her a shake, I could see the leading edge of it. Poor thing, it was a bad one, like something cooked up between Mobil and the Exxon Valdez. It didn't help that Linda was already a walking offence in Claudia's book, whose other specialities included throwing Year 7 kids into lockers and slamming the door.

Anyway, Linda began to cry, and I shifted uneasily as she wailed, 'Why won't you guys ever leave me alone?' It was a good question. Shame there would never be an answer.

Linda snivelled harder. 'Was g-gunna w-wash it off, if you let me…'

Claudia showed her teeth, light glinting off her super-stay-on lip gloss. 'So now's your chance.'

She set Linda down, almost gently. Linda hesitated, then tried to push past the wedge of girls blocking the door. Neither of them, built like a pack of perfectly coiffed frost-free refrigerators, gave an inch. Standing just behind Sharys, her French manicure still digging into my arm, I realised with a sinking heart what Claudia had in mind. She was so predictable.

'Uh, excuse me,' Linda added, gesturing helplessly at the sinks beyond us.

Claudia laughed, moving forward so the backs of Linda's legs pressed against the toilet bowl. '*Excuse you* is right, Jelly Belly. Where you going? Water's *right there*. So start washing.'

Linda gaped, finally comprehending. Seeing no way out, she began to scoop and cry, scoop and cry, while Claudia, Sharys and *Cadence? Rhapsody? Prelude?* almost wet themselves laughing. All the while, the sound Linda was making as she scrubbed at her bloody skirt with toilet water made my skin crawl. I tried to pull out of Sharys' grasp. In reply, she just dug her nails in harder.

But then something really strange happened.

Linda was still sobbing and scooping water out of the dunny with her bare hands when a message appeared on the mirror opposite the stall. I saw it first out of the corner of my eye, then Sharys—who'd felt the shock run up the muscles of my arm—turned. Suddenly, everyone went quiet.

She is You, the message said.

They looked like words you write in the fog that appears on a mirror after a scalding shower. They were clear and distinct for a moment, then they faded. But we'd all read the message, which had got to Claudia's two goons, who'd gone white.

'You do that?' Claudia said sharply, looking at me. I shook my head, pointing numbly at Sharys' big hand, still curled around my arm, like a claw.

Confused, Linda started crying again, and the sound infuriated Claudia so much that she backhanded her across the face to shut her up. The sound of flesh on flesh shocked everyone motionless once more, including Linda, who was standing in a puddle of bloodstained water, her wet skirt and white socks stained pink, her mouth a round *O*.

Claudia's blue eyes narrowed dangerously. 'If I find out one of you has been taking the piss, especially you...' She pulled a fistful of my jumper close for a moment. *'I'll have you.'*

Then she stormed out of the toilet, not bothering to wait for her backup, who filed out in wordless confusion a second later. Which left Linda and me standing there—hot tears misting up the backs of Linda's lenses, snot running down over her mouth and chin.

I helped clean Linda up as much as I could, as much as I could bear to touch her. Even helped her dry her pink socks and skirt under the automatic dryer before I remembered I was seriously busting and locked myself in a cubicle. Linda had been so ashamed, or so grateful, that she hadn't been able to string a complete sentence together and had beaten it as soon as the coast was clear. When I was finally alone, I exhaled, wondering what was around the corner, because something was coming like a freight train, it had to be.

I knew who'd written that message.

'You there?' I said wearily, pants around my ankles, studying the ceiling as though Eve might be hiding up there, like the outline of the Virgin Mary. 'You there?'

✦

I was at my desk that night, my back to the room, thinking about that strange look Jordan had given me, when I began to smell flowers.

I didn't turn immediately, crossing my arms to stop myself from shaking. 'This has got to *stop*,' I insisted in a low voice. 'School's hard enough without adding something like you to the mix. Haven't I done enough?'

But I could feel her just standing there behind me, waiting. Patient and inexorable as time.

Turning away from my open laptop, finally, I got the same electric jolt I felt the other times I'd seen her. She looked so much like Mum it brought the sting of tears to my eyes.

Impassive, unmoving, Eve showed me a rundown house called *Hatherlea*.

That was it. Just an image of a sprawling Victorian weatherboard—with a prominent nameplate—that probably used to be a pretty, sunny yellow but was now just an all-over diseased grey. I saw an overgrown garden of long grass and sky-high feral roses, rusting ironwork on the verandah, no one moving in or around the house. There was junk mail frozen like a sodden waterfall coming out of a letterbox set into a low, red brick fence that had half toppled over into the garden behind it.

'Thanks for nothing, Eve,' I said fiercely after she flashed the image at me a couple more times for good measure. Same thing, same camera angles. 'This is the last one, okay? After this, you leave me alone. You rest in peace and never come back.'

By way of an answer, she just winked out like a light. *Over to you, Storkie*, she pretty much said.

5

How Eve found these people I was supposed to help was beyond me. Basket cases, most of them. People I wouldn't even notice if she didn't tell me they were there. There was definitely a pattern. The people Eve wanted me to find were all pretty badly, um, the nicest way to put it was...*dented*.

Hatherlea. It was like the name of a house you'd find in one of those set texts for English. I never knew what those books were about and I never enjoyed them, and that pretty much summed up my search for that house and everything that came afterwards.

I couldn't sleep after Eve had shown me *Hatherlea*. Searching the internet at 4.21 in the morning for it didn't improve my mood. Try Googling the word and see what comes up. A dentist, a guesthouse, an art gallery. A playwright, a porn star, a logistics manager. *Hatter Lee, Heather Lee*—every combination except the one I actually wanted. Pages and pages of bum steers. It was hopeless.

By the time Gran was up and strapped firmly into her Dr Rey's shapewear, I still had no clue where Eve wanted me to go or what I was supposed to do when I got there.

'You okay, love?' Gran asked over a heavily loaded ham, cheese and tomato toastie. She still couldn't believe how she'd turned on the mid-morning news yesterday and seen grainy replay footage of *me*—shot on someone's phone— saving some old codger's life. He hadn't been grateful. He'd called me all sorts of terrible names that were edited out of the news stories as the paramedics worked on his face. Hey, he'd had to land on something.

The police had arrested the driver a couple of suburbs away. He'd probably had similar work done to his profile because, apparently, he'd resisted arrest in a *big* way. Pre-existing rap sheet longer than my arm. Eve had me mixing with interesting company.

'My girl, the hero. Still don't know what you were doing out there, but I'm glad you were. You did good, love.' Gran gave me a quick, embarrassed squeeze and looked hard into my face, telling me I was looking peaky and could have the day off school if I needed it.

Perfect. It was like Eve had set it all up.

'If I wanted to find a house called *Hatherlea*,' I asked Gran casually as she tipped leftovers out of the recyclables into a bucket and put some elbow grease into wiping down the scarred main bar, 'how would I go about doing it?'

'Now why'd you want to do *that*?' Gran said, raising her eyebrows. Good question. Hadn't thought it through before I opened my big mouth.

I back-pedalled furiously. No one had twigged to the Crime Stoppers call I'd made with that kid's mum yet, or connected it with me saving the old bastard on Sunday, but I didn't want even Gran to know about Eve. It was all too hard to go into without sounding insane and she already watched me, like a hawk, when she thought I wasn't looking.

'History assignment,' I babbled. 'Important landmarks of early Melbourne. Since I've got the day off—cheers—I want to try and find it, maybe take some shots for my project, but I can't remember the street name. Just the name of the house, silly me. It's old. Very, very old.' I held my breath, feeling dishonest.

Gran's face cleared. 'Well, love,' she said reaching under the countertop and feeling around. She pushed an old street directory across at me and sailed off to the kitchen to try and impose her will over Cook about the day's menu.

I knew she would lose, but hope sprang eternal with Gran.

There was only one *Hatherlea Street* in the book. It had to be a good place to start since the name was so unusual. And a pretty expensive one to reach, too, once I figured out I'd have to hop a tram, a train and a bus to get to what might not even be the right place. But I had all day now. And there were worse things to do, I supposed, than trek all over town doing one final good deed for a genuine, paid-up member of the Undead. Who got to put that on their CV?

✦

I got off the bus someplace that had to be the farthest I'd ever travelled from home before on my own. Usually, I lived my whole life within walking distance of The Star. It was a real eye opener.

Hatherlea Street was the absolute heart of darkness, the outer, outer north-eastern 'burbs, practically a different universe. It ran off a street that ran off the poor excuse for a main road I was standing on. I stopped into a milk bar for a fried dimmie to fortify my nerves, then I started properly looking.

In the end, it was pretty easy to find. Almost like Eve had pre-planned the entire operation, which, in a sense, she had. *Hatherlea*—more an old homestead than a house—was on a massive block at least the size of three ordinary gardens knocked together. Turned out the street was named *after* the house, not the other way around, and if that house wasn't already haunted up the wazoo before I set foot in it, I'd be laughing.

In real life, in the harsh autumnal light, the house looked even worse than Eve had made out, if that was possible. Half the trees in the frontyard were actually dead and parts of the guttering hung down like a rusting sort of exotic creeper, a decorative feature that dovetailed nicely with the missing wooden floorboards in the return verandah. The roof was missing a few slate tiles and the cement walkways were badly buckled and overgrown with weeds. There were bedsheets hanging in most of the windows in place of curtains. Good housekeeping did not figure highly in the life of whoever owned this joint.

No one could possibly be living here, I told myself, the last bit of the dimmie sticking in my throat.

Trying to get a better handle on the problem, I walked up and down the street a couple of times. I swore a curtain twitched here and there but no one bailed me up to ask me what I was doing. Save for *Hatherlea* itself, it was a pretty ordinary street. Nineteen-seventies brown brick places mostly. Neat, neat gardens. Lace netting in the windows. Lots of roller guards. Probably all built on *Hatherlea's* old grounds.

It was almost 1pm. I'd been procrastinating for at least half an hour. The pointing finger of God had not appeared to tell me what to do. So I went in, finally, even though the house had *trouble* written all over it. I jumped the rusty front gate and walked up the buckling footpath to the front door.

Of course there would be no doorbell. Just a heavy lion's head doorknocker that had half rusted shut. I tapped that a couple of times, waited a polite interval, then started bashing the crap out of it. Still nothing. I was not going to get into *Hatherlea* by the official entrance, that much was obvious.

I rounded the side of the house, skirting fallen tree branches, abandoned pet-food bowls, cracked coils of garden hose, a marble birdbath filled with evil smelling water—a muddy, browny-green, kind of like my eyes.

At the back, the Victorian sash windows looked solid and impenetrable and welded shut. I didn't fancy breaking in through one of those, figuring that the point of this exercise couldn't possibly involve me and a stint in a juvenile detention centre. Eve couldn't want that, I wouldn't be any use to her in the lock-up. Still, really starting to sweat now, I told myself to just take a peek inside then call for backup. There was something about the whole set-up that had my skin crawling.

Heading up a set of cement stairs, I noticed a screen

door ajar and a pet flap built into the back door. Kneeling down, I pushed the flap in cautiously and *the most disgusting odour I have ever detected in my life* wafted back out of the darkness through the gap.

It was piss and shit and worse, all rolled up. Like the toilets at the footy, or The Star after an international soccer final, except left to stew for days on end—no, *years*. I let the flap fall back and sat down hard on the top step, gasping for air.

'What do you want me to *do*, Eve?' I gagged. 'Clean up? *Jesus*.'

Part of me argued, pretty persuasively, that I should just call for backup now and get the hell out of there. And then what? It was never that simple. I wasn't supposed to be there just to observe. That was Eve's job. I was her hands, her body, her go-to girl.

Shuddering, I stood up and tried the back door. And, bloody hell, it *opened*.

✦

I took a deep breath and entered what must have been the kitchen, where the smell was so bad that I had to take my jumper off and tie it around my face. There were plates of rotten food piled up high on the kitchen table, around the sink, cups full of swampy liquid, mould climbing the ends of the kitchen curtains, the fruit in the fruit bowl, piles of actual *shit* everywhere.

As I tiptoed through to the hallway, trying hard not to touch anything, there was a sudden loud sound of scattering and I rocked back in fear until I figured it must be animals of some kind. Rats? Cats? I relaxed. They didn't bother me so much—I'd encountered them often enough in the cellar at home. Maybe meeting Eve had toughened me up more than I knew.

Weak sunlight filtered in through the bedsheets over the windows in the rooms that led off the hall. I could see some of the old furniture looked really beautiful, but the effect was spoilt by that overwhelming smell of shit and rot and worse that was cut through with a top note of… *maybe something dead?*

A chill flashed across my skin. Maybe that was why I was here. I reached into my pack and gripped my mobile phone, ready to do the deed—whatever the hell it was— and run, run away.

As I crossed into the front part of the house I saw it. The body of an old woman, surrounded by cats, more than a dozen of them, like a furry guard of honour. She was lying facedown on the carpet in the doorway of a front bedroom. It was piled high with old newspapers, magazines, boxed-up records, folded paper shopping bags in their thousands, an army of lined-up shoes and hatboxes, rolls of unused toilet paper in baskets. If there was a reason for it all, it escaped me. You could barely see the unmade double bed, like a lonely ship under cover of a knitted afghan blanket, bobbing in the midst of that sea of crap.

I didn't want to touch her, I thought she was long gone, that her cats were keeping her cold body company and I should just make my anonymous call to 000 and beat it. But as I got closer, the cats reared and spat as one, like a living wave, and I realised it was worse than that, they were beginning to *eat* her to stay alive: there was fresh, bright blood all over the back of the woman's legs where they'd begun to gnaw.

I am not ashamed to say that I untied the jumper from around my face and vomited.

✦

Time sped up after that. I beat the cats off, screaming like a hysterical banshee, and turned the woman over before calling an ambulance and wrenching the front door open for some air, any air—anything to replace the stinking fug inside the house. And I propped her up a bit, and talked to her, and covered her with that disgusting, hair-covered afghan blanket, all the while thinking she was already dead, and what was I doing here, what had Eve been thinking? Would the police think I'd done it? And before I knew it, a pair of them charged up the footpath towards me, fingers pointing, shouting, *Hold it right there, young lady, we want a word with you*, and even though I hadn't done anything, the thought that I would go to jail froze me on the spot.

Somehow, she was still alive. They told me later it was a cocktail of port and medication, old age and malnutrition, and if I'd waited even half an hour more the cats could've had her. It was *that* close.

Turned out, the neighbours really *had* called the police when they'd spotted me skulking around the old lady's place and I'd called emergency services, which equalled one big, fat circus when everyone arrived, sirens screaming. Hatherlea Street had never seen anything like it.

Imagine Gran's surprise when she turned on the Tuesday evening news. Some hard-nosed journo had even managed to dig up the Crime Stoppers call I'd made with that kid's mum, which made *me*—for that day at least— bigger than, I dunno, *Brangelina*.

6

While I'd been wagging school to save the old woman—who turned out to be a reclusive, cat-collecting miser, with a fortune in gold bars buried in her back garden—word of the miracle that had happened in the girls' toilets had filtered everywhere.

Of course, even if I'd been at school I would have had no idea what people were saying about me because I never really know what's going on. Like how skirts were suddenly short again this year and knee-highs were back, whereas last year all the girls I knew had been wearing long skirts and anklets, thin black Alice bands and yellow nail polish. When the wind changed and brought the scent of distant danger to the herd, I just never felt it.

Anyway, Linda Jelly may have been the weakest link in the Ivy Street food chain, but even *she* had friends. In my absence, her friends had told their friends who told their friends that psychic Storkie Teague had somehow done it again—right on school grounds this time. She'd made spooky-arse writing appear on the wall and it'd scared the living crap out of the toughest bitches at Ivy Street High. Which meant that Claudia P. and her best mates were gunning for me, and the three of them grabbed me the moment I stepped back onto school property the morning after the *Hatherlea* incident and locked me in the gymnasium storeroom for a personal touch-up.

The teachers at Ivy Street were deaf, dumb and blind, or they liked to see scientific principles, the law of the jungle, in action. Despite the fact I was screaming my head off, no one heard, saw or remembered me being bundled through the gym by the Gang of Three just before the bell rang. I was doomed.

'How'd you do that?' Claudia said pleasantly, referring to the message Eve had helpfully posted on the mirror. Like no time at all had passed, Sharys reattached herself to the nerves of my left elbow, and fear began to take wing through my body again like a trapped bird.

Harmonica, or whatever she was called, moved into guard position in front of the door as Claudia commenced massaging a balled-up fist like a professional prizefighter readying to defend the heavyweight crown. I knew I'd be lucky if I left school today with the same face. But Claudia was smarter than that; she'd monstered more people than I'd had hot dinners. So she didn't aim high, she just punched me in the guts, a quick one, two. I went down on all fours and rolled over, seeing purple and retching.

So that was to be the *modus operandi*. No visible bruising. I'd just be unable to sit, stand or eat for a while.

There were to be no miracles from me today; that was clear. Claudia administered a painful nipple cripple while I was down and that was the signal for everyone to pile on, kicking me in the ribs, the guts, the chest, the pelvis.

'She's got a lower pain threshold,' I heard someone snort, 'than even Linda Jelly.' I think I blacked out in record time.

And before I knew it, I'd woken in a puddle of my own mucus to the sight of Jordan Haig looking down on me. As I stared at him through a fog of hot tears, it occurred to me that maybe I'd died and what I was seeing was the last crazed imaginings of my almost lifeless brain. But then he crouched down and touched me, and I flinched. Instantly, pain began to sing again through my body.

The three stooges were long gone. It was just him and me among the gym mats and it was like my deepest nightmare had come to pass. *Jordan Haig*, the most beautiful guy this side of Floyd Parker, here in the gymnasium storeroom. Alone, too, as if guided by satellite, a strange look on his face. What was he doing here?

'You, uh, okay?'

He sounded uncomfortable, almost awkward. He helped me to sit up as I wiped my face on the back of my sleeve, and I numbly registered that, for five seconds at least, we'd been holding hands. Now if that wasn't miraculous, then nothing was.

I was too beat up to speak, and for a moment I could have been Linda Jelly: ashamed to be seen this way, but so abjectly grateful at the same time. When I was finally on my feet, Jordan backed away with his hands up in a curious gesture of surrender. It was like something you'd see partway through an old Saturday afternoon Western, where the guy under the white flag approaches the enemy, delivers his message, then retreats, hoping he won't be shot in the back. I'd never seen Jordan so uneasy, almost like he was afraid of *me*, and it made a tiny bit of my bashed-in brain take notice.

He waited for me to stumble out behind him then shut the storeroom door behind us. 'We're nothing,' he muttered, not looking me in the eye. 'I don't know how much you can do, or what you want, but it goes no further, okay?'

Before I could even start to frame an answer to any of that, he walked off with his head down and his hands in his pockets.

He sure knows what to say to a girl, I thought, the floor ducking and weaving under my feet.

✦

'What's wrong with you?' snapped Mrs McKendry at me as I huddled in the back row, nursing a balled-up, bloody tissue. It was the third period of the day and I'd already suffered stoically through Biology, my eyes on the back of Jordan Haig's head as he gave an intelligent, off-the-cuff summary of what an onion epidermis actually did. He'd put his words straight into practice, his eyes skimming straight past mine as we'd all taken our seats.

We were truly nothing. That hurt almost more than my ribs did.

I was trying to put it all together—how had he come to be there?—but none of the pieces fit. They weren't even from the same puzzle. And now Mrs McKendry was trying to get me to solve a probability question before a live audience—who almost certainly knew what Claudia and her goons had done to me. It was humiliating. I couldn't hold my head up properly and my nose had started to bleed. Stress sometimes brings on nosebleeds with me, which just added to my general, dazzling allure.

'We all know what *you've* been up to, Sophie,' Mrs McKendry added hatefully, 'you busy little Samaritan. But that doesn't excuse you from telling me what proportion of smarties in that cone full of smarties is likely to be *blue*.' She drew a ring around the complicated looking diagram of a cone (r = 100 cm) that she'd drawn up on the whiteboard.

Blue smarties? At a freakin' time like this?

A feeling rose up in me that was pretty close to white-hot, exterminate-anything-in-my-path rage. It was a weird sensation: I was almost high with anger. My hands were shaking as I gathered up my books. She could take that cone and its load of flipping smarties of many colours, I told myself, and—

Knowing I'd pay for it later in a million different horrible ways, I just left the room. Even surprised myself. Held my head up as far as my neck would let me and staggered out the door.

To my amazement, no one tried to stop me, though it was a sea of open mouths, wall-to-wall. Biddy had told me that there was still a rumour going around after Monday's phenomenon-in-the-toilets that I might have somehow developed super powers. The *Hatherlea* thing had only intensified the speculation. So even Mrs McKendry let me pass without a word.

Jordan Haig and I came face-to-face in the deserted second floor corridor where all the Year 12s had their lockers.

What he was doing there, I did not know, but we had to stop meeting like this. It was bad for my heart. I took a breath that hurt right down to my toes.

He did a double take at the exact same moment, shooting me a look of such pure loathing that I almost recoiled.

How did I deserve *that*?

He snarled, 'I can see her, you know. And I know what she's trying to do.'

The words set off fresh shocks in my system.

'You tell her to keep away from me.'

That's when I realised Eve was standing right behind me looking at him looking at me. And she was *smiling*.

Shit, he could see her. She'd suddenly chosen to reappear right here, right now, and he could *see* her?

'You can see her?' I gasped, forgetting that Jordan and I were nothing and shouldn't even be speaking.

Why was Eve smiling?

It didn't make her look any more…human. If anything, the look on her face was almost greedy. Whatever it was, it wasn't an expression of joy, nothing as simple as that.

Jordan's look was utterly disparaging. 'Of course I can see her.' He grabbed his pack and skateboard and slammed his locker door. '*You never let them in*, or this is what happens.'

'You mean, all this time…' I scrambled for words, for understanding.

'Whatever she wants, tell her I'm not interested,' Jordan shot back, averting his gaze. He pressed his fingers into the skin of his left arm fiercely, from shoulder to wrist, before hitching his pack higher.

Why was he so agitated? And what was he talking about? What would Eve want with him when she had me? Suddenly, I had so many questions I couldn't get them out fast enough. But Jordan was already walking away.

'Wait, wait!' I shouted at his back. '*You* tell her. She doesn't speak to *me*. She doesn't even *smile* at me. She just makes me do things. Why? *Why?*'

Jordan just hunched his shoulders and kept walking, which is when the haunting of Jordan Haig officially began.

I watched, open-mouthed, as lockers erupted as he passed, their contents exploding outwards in step with Jordan's departure but somehow never hitting him. It was like he moved in a protective bubble or force-field as he wedged his skateboard under one armpit and pressed and pressed on his arms; the left first, then the right. Exercise books, rulers, runners, folders, phones, diaries—all seemed to change course before they could touch him.

The incredible noise caused classroom doors up and down the corridor to shoot open in time for everyone to get a load of their personal belongings raining down from the sky. With me just standing there like a stunned mullet, at the far end.

Of course, by then, Jordan was gone and there was nothing I could say that anyone would believe except, maybe, *Abracadabra?*

✦

The point where the principal sent me home—after telling me not to darken the doors of the school for a week—was the point where The Star Hotel officially came under siege.

Just after the first evening news bulletin, a whole lot of rubber-neckers who never usually went near a pub—you could spot people like that a mile off—came in to see me pour drinks at the bar like I could turn beer into solid gold. As the hours wore on, regulars couldn't achieve the corner of a bar stool, let alone a table. Gran was even forced to put two hired gorillas on the door and institute a red velvet rope to keep the hopefuls in line. A red velvet rope. Like my life had suddenly turned into the hottest VIP nightclub in town, because they'd all come to see *me*.

I winced as the TV over the bar proclaimed me *The Saviour of Sancerre Street* and flashed up a street view of The Star. 'Talk is,' a female reporter said brightly from right outside, 'a busload of pilgrims from Far North Queensland is planning to drop by the pub after seeing the Pope conduct a public mass at the racecourse next month.

They're bringing sick babies and cancer sufferers. Hoping Sophie "Storkie" Teague will "lay on the hands" and see if anything happens. Back to you, Garry.'

'Imagine,' Gran slung at me dryly as we pulled beers back-to-back, barely able to keep up with the orders, 'the Pope and you, on a double bill.'

'I'd come and watch if that happened,' Dirty Neil said, licking his lips as I passed just out of his reach with an inward shudder. 'Make a day of it.'

Gran gave him the stink eye as she swiped his empty glass off the counter. 'The idea! She couldn't heal a cold sore if she tried.' She addressed the wall of faces pressed up closest to the bar. 'The Council's even called me about permit issues and taking out extra insurance if we decide to go ahead with a—what did they call it?—*public blessing*. And did I tell you how much I hate the paparazzi? They've stuffed the neighbourhood up good and proper. You can't drive anywhere without a bedsheet over your head with holes cut out in it for your eyes.'

As people laughed, someone yelled out, 'Love!' trying to climb up over the countertop, 'Give us a selfie?'

I shook my head.

'Lay on the hands? I'd love a laying on of the hands.'

'Got no tits or bum to speak of, does she?'

Panicked, I backed away as people kept calling out and filming me with their cameras right out in front of my face. But there was nowhere to go behind the bar and I yelled, 'Gran?'

I could hear Linda Jelly unloading on live TV about the endemic bully culture at Ivy Street High. The reporter cut next to Claudia P., who said primly on camera through shiny pink lips that Sophie Teague was a known Satan worshipper. Mrs McKendry added eagerly that I was easily the worst student she'd ever taught in her twenty-three years of maths teaching. 'And to make matters worse, she's extremely *insolent*.'

Gran was saying, '…And I've had a gutful of people trying to sneak in claiming they're delivery boys or C-list Aussie soap stars! We've even had reporters going through our rubbish for evidence that Soph's "special".'

'Gran?'

'…And I've told every celebrity manager that's called to *bugger off* in five different ways. Said I won't start living off my only grandchild like a maggot until I'm at least eighty and demented…'

'*GRAN?*' I bawled, my voice loud and shaky. And, I swear, the entire room stopped dead.

Gran turned, mid-sentence, took one look at my face and said, 'Right, this is not a zoo and she's not an exhibit for everyone's delectation.' She flapped the end of her black apron at me. '*You*, go upstairs. You lot, if you're not drinking—the door's over there.'

The raucous laughter of strangers followed me up the stairs. The one bright point of my night was that no one seemed to know about Jordan's involvement, mainly because he didn't appear to be talking to anyone about anything. And I was glad about that, because the way I was feeling, I didn't really want to find out his opinion of me over free-to-air.

The hoopla about me was even bigger than the city shooting that had set everything in motion and brought Eve into my life in the first place. That story had been huge—*Imagine that happening, here! In this town!* The headlines had screamed for days: *Ice! Vodka shooters! Bikers! Strippers! Roid Rage!*

But my story was bigger, because it was an excuse for every wacko psychic spoon-bending medium to come out of the woodwork with their take on things. Somehow, they were linking me to the Kennedy assassinations, recent sightings of alien spacecraft in the Northern Territory and a serial killer that had been plaguing Western Australia for decades. It was wild.

The sceptics were having a field day, too. Everyone suddenly had an opinion on Storkie Teague. The best was when some ex-Department of Defence genius said over the radio talkback, which Cook insisted on having on in the kitchen, that they should hook me up to a stealth bomber and have me end the War on Terror single-handedly.

The irony of it was that what Eve had done to my life had pushed her own story right out of the press, and there was no one I could tell that to.

✦

Eve had been lying low since that afternoon's fireworks at school but at 1.27am she appeared in my bedroom. Gran had just gone to bed for the night, the place was dark, and only two of the major networks still had a news van parked outside. It was as good a time as any to talk, if that's what you could call it.

I had to try to remember to keep my voice down. 'You go *away*,' I hissed, ticking off on my fingers. 'The kid, the old guy and the cat woman: third time's supposed to be a charm, according to the Book of Joss. I've done enough. All this attention is the exact opposite of what I am about.'

My reputation had taken a real hammering at Ivy Street since the locker Armageddon had occurred. After I'd regained the safety of my bedroom, Biddy Cole had called me to relay breathlessly that the Christian Students Group—that holds prayer meetings every Tuesday lunchtime—was putting together a petition to have me expelled for being a practising witch. She usually only called me when there was no one else left to spread gossip to. It had an extra dimension of weirdness to have it be about *me*.

Eve listened to me rant, stony-faced, then did something she's never done before. She turned her back on me, mid-sentence, and walked straight through my bedroom door.

Despite everything, I was impressed.

I sat and stared at the door after that for ages. She didn't reappear. *Okay,* I thought, *that's it then.* And I thought it was. I actually breathed out. So she'd come to say *Goodbye.* Job done.

But something still made me get up and open the door. I got the shock of my life when I saw her standing at the end of the upstairs hallway, gleaming. She'd been waiting for me.

She'd never moved much in my presence before now. Maybe she was getting stronger. I liked to think of her as more passive-aggressive than direct action, but here she was, practically jiggling on the spot.

While I continued to stand there, paralysed, she began to wink in and out with an almost urgent rhythm. As I watched, she reappeared on the lower landing, just beside the jukebox where the stairs turned and went down into the corridor near the public washrooms. Then she flickered back into sight at the end of the hallway, doing that twice more until I realised she was asking me to follow her. Every hair on my body must have risen in horror. It was *dark* outside.

Eve flickered back into sight on the jukebox landing

then reappeared at the end of the hall. *Flick* then back. *Flick* then back, the movements growing so fast she was almost a blur. I inhaled shakily, suddenly getting it. She was pleading with me the only way she knew how. How often had I been voiceless myself? How often had I needed someone just to stop and take notice and ask me what it was that I really wanted?

For a fleeting second, I also grasped the message Eve had been trying to convey to Claudia P. in the upper girls' toilets. Eve was my mother. She was me. Eve's story could be my own: *Girl goes missing, nobody gives*. It wasn't really about what Eve wanted me to *do*. It was about me working out what had happened to her to make her this way. Light bulb moment. Nobody could do the job but me, dark or no dark, because nobody was looking for her now; I'd made sure of that.

'Wait! Wait!' I called out softly, grabbing a hoodie, jamming on my socks and runners and sticking a flashlight into the pocket of my trackies because I don't glow or see in the dark the way Eve can.

7

Sensibly, Eve did her next disappearing trick right through the back door of The Star, which leads to a narrow, cobbled laneway that runs up the back of the pub and the six rundown, double-storey Victorian terrace houses next door. We were out of Sancerre Lane and turning out of Sancerre Street before any of the overweight newsmen in the parked media vans would have had any idea we were gone.

If you didn't count Eve—and I didn't, because talking to her was like talking to a stone—it actually felt pretty great being out on my own. Everything I'd done lately had seemed to come complete with a rent-a-crowd, or an emotionally damaging brush-off from Jordan Haig.

Eve disappeared and reappeared in the dark between

the streetlights ahead of me, first on this side of the road, then the other. She knew the streets like a local, taking a shortcut through Edinburgh Gardens—which are seriously scary after dark—and hot-footing it, if you could call it that, right through the Holden Street Reserve and up the Park Street Trail. I swear, if you'd seen the back of her moving along, you'd have thought she was a person like you and me, just on a mission. I'd never seen her so, well, animated.

We'd soon crossed over into Carlton North, staying well clear of the General Cemetery and Princes Park, and entered the fringes of Brunswick East. Even at this hour, traffic along Sydney Road was steady and I put my hoodie up and my head down, hoping no one would try to approach me. I wrapped one hand around the torch in my pocket for good measure. People had contract hits taken out on them around here. They made TV dramas about people who lived in this area that no one in this area could actually watch until a judge cleared it first. A disembodied woman like Eve wasn't going to offer me much protection.

After the first few blocks, it began to rain heavily and I started to lose all feeling in my hands and face. As we ducked left up a side street, I knew we'd long since crossed over into Brunswick and were moving in the direction of

Coburg, maybe Pascoe Vale South, but the street signs had begun to blur and I was getting really tired. I don't know where Eve goes when she's not with me, but she never seemed to need any rest. And the rain didn't trouble her much either.

The street that we finally came to looked like any other street in the area: narrow Victorian terraces built right up against Mediterranean-inspired 1950s places bursting with concrete, columns and fruit trees, or houses that were a curious combination of both, as if one era had begun steadily cannibalising the other.

The house Eve stopped across the road from was one of the latter: a single-fronted Victorian that had had every trace of its Victorian-ness painstakingly ripped out and replaced with something modern and jarring. Roller guards instead of shutters, sliding windows with aluminium frames instead of graceful bay ones, plaster columns instead of iron lacework, all flanked by potted citrus trees. It was sensationally ugly, but well kept. The concrete driveway was weed-free and everything in the yard—from the rolled-up extension hose to the box hedging—was immaculate. A single light was on in the front room; otherwise the house was in darkness.

I looked sideways at Eve enquiringly. As the rain finally thinned, then stopped, she stood still for a long time, just facing the house, like she was thinking. When I crossed the street to get a better look, she didn't follow me. I'd done several passes of the front of the house on my own before I realised, stupid from the cold and the long walk, that Eve either couldn't, or wouldn't, come any closer. I crossed back to where she was, the dim light from an overhead streetlamp passing just faintly *through* her.

'So what's the deal?' I said, unable to keep the weariness out of my voice. 'What do you want me to do this time?'

Would it be crazy cat lady all over again? I wondered. Or something even worse?

Eve continued to stare at the house with a strange expression that I hadn't seen before. There was something almost vulnerable in her usually unreadable features. She turned to me finally, looking as if she would at last actually *speak*, but instead she held out her hand to me, which made me hold out mine.

Into my palm fell something almost weightless and icy. Beautiful, but unusual, too. It was a wide, beaten gold ring, with the outline of a sleeping woman's face on it, the band carved to resemble the tresses of her long hair.

And then Eve just vanished.

◆

I stared at the thing for a while, turning it over and over in my hand.

It was almost three in the morning and I knew that Eve's stuff could never wait. She always did things for a reason—admittedly, one only *she* knew about—but there was never time built in to muck around. She was all business, and I knew, without a doubt, that she wanted me to give this ring to the person inside that house. The light was still on, almost as if they were waiting for me. There was no coming back and doing it later. I might never be able to find this place again on my own. There was never a later with Eve. It had to be now, because now was all she had.

So I took a deep breath and crossed back over, vaulting the low, iron gate and walking quickly and quietly up the slick front footpath. Concrete was good that way. I'd made my way up the path and onto the speckled verandah and I still hadn't made a sound. Eve couldn't have done better than me in approaching that house. But still I hesitated, studying the tiny orange light beneath the electronic doorbell. There was no name written on the nameplate. How would I address whoever opened the door? This was loony.

But it was *all* loony, and what was the worst the person could do? I asked myself. Call the police? I'd just drop the ring at their feet and run. Mission accomplished. It wasn't as if you could be arrested for giving someone pretty jewellery. Still, as I pressed the doorbell, the adrenaline that suddenly flooded into my brain made me see stars and my heartbeat kick up. There could be guns. I still didn't know what I was going to say or do, and it was too late to figure it out now.

I was just about to press the buzzer a second time when the door opened wide enough to reveal a single dark-brown eye above a low-slung security chain.

'What you want?' the eye addressed me suspiciously.

There was no going back.

'Someone wanted me to give this to you,' I said, holding the ring up to the gap in the door. The eye moved closer, squinted, opened wide. The door slammed shut.

I was debating whether to leave the gold band on the doormat when I heard the sound of running footsteps, the security chain rattling. Then the door flew open. And, I swear, the woman's anguish and turmoil hit me like a *wave*. I could feel it and I actually fell back.

The eye belonged to a tiny woman in a dressing gown and slippers. Italian? Greek? Long, dark hair unbound, silver winding through it at the temples. Deep lines down her face. But she wasn't *old* old. Maybe a few years younger than Gran. But she looked like she'd been sick or something. She wore every year of her age on her face, and then some.

She had one hand jammed into her mouth and the other one gripped tightly around a large silver crucifix that she was shaking at me like you would shake water off an umbrella. As she forced me back off the verandah with it, she cried out in some language I couldn't understand, short, sharp sentences ringing out in the biting air.

'Look,' I said, when she drew breath to begin her incantations all over again, 'I just wanted to give it to you. I'll leave it right here, okay?'

I raised both my hands high over my head to show her that I meant no harm, then proceeded to place the ring down on the footpath, exaggerating my movements.

The woman began to lower her crucifix. I was just glad she'd stopped screaming, afraid she'd wake the neighbours and land me right back on *Today Tonight*.

The woman stared down at the ring like it was a coiled snake on the footpath, something sent to test her. She looked almost too afraid to touch it—faint with fear—but as I watched, she passed the crucifix over it shakily, prodded the ring with her slippered foot as if it had the power to burn her flesh.

'It's quite real,' I said. 'Don't worry.' I backed slowly away from her towards the gate; glad I'd got the job done. I was really tired. I wanted to be home in my room with my doona right up over my nose—even if it meant that I had to have Eve watch me sleep.

'And you?' the woman suddenly croaked, looking up at me, the crucifix like some weird extension of her right hand. 'You real?'

The question caught me by surprise and I nodded.

'Of course I am.'

Too real, I thought. *Boringly real. As real as. Too real for all this.*

The woman frowned, studying me so intently her head was tilted to one side. 'The one she give this to you, she real, too?'

I didn't know how to answer that. As I hesitated, the tiny woman bent and snatched the ring up off the footpath.

As she closed her fingers around that slender band, she burst into noisy tears, hugging the thing to her chest and rocking on her heels, back and forth, as she wailed and beat herself with it.

I got the hell out of there as fast as my legs would carry me. I'm no good with grief, just ask Gran.

✦

The next day, no surprises, I had a cold.

I was still in bed at noon when Biddy Cole rang me again on my mobile to tell me the astonishing news that *Jordan Haig* had officially been given a week off school as well. *Effective immediately.*

The news made me sit up right away. 'Why?' I asked, wondering at the sudden, weird symmetries in our lives; why his name kept cropping up when before I couldn't have bribed anyone to say it in my hearing.

'Because everywhere he is today totally becomes a walking disaster zone about five seconds later!' Biddy said with relish. 'People are saying either *you're* doing it by remote control or *he's* the one behind the weird stuff that's been going on and you're just the patsy.'

'I'm not doing anything that doesn't involve a box of tissues,' I said with a tissue stuffed firmly up one nostril. 'You can quote me on that.' And I knew Biddy would, too, being the fastest mouth in the Western world. 'What do you mean, *disaster zone?*'

Biddy proceeded to list everything that had gone wrong around Jordan Haig since I'd been banned from school yesterday. 'He set off the automatic sprinkler system in the science wing for starters,' she breathed. 'Fire engines came. *Three.*'

'That would be his personal magnetism at work,' I giggled. 'Too hot to handle. What else?'

'Speaking of which,' Biddy exclaimed, 'he then proceeded to set fire to his art class *after* the engines had left! Most of the Year 12 sculptures in the next room went up in flames. You can imagine they aren't too happy about *that*. Stav Heliotis is threatening physical retribution, tatts or no tatts. Plus, mice invaded the staffroom. People standing on chairs, you name it.'

You could hear the wonder in Biddy's voice. I sincerely hoped that Mrs McKendry and her pastel cashmere twin set had been present for that one.

'And it doesn't stop there!' Biddy breathed. '*Two* of the bookshelves in the library collapsed as he walked by, almost taking out Mr Moore and 7A who were doing a research project around the other side. The second floor boys' toilets flooded after Jordan went in to wash his hands. Stuff like that! Reporters, cops, everything have been crawling all over. Biggest thing to happen since you pulled that locker stunt.'

'That wasn't me,' I replied, distracted by what I'd heard and forgetting how no one was supposed to know about that. 'Jordan was there, too.'

Armed with that added bit of dirt, Biddy rang off. I couldn't begin to imagine what people were saying about me, about him, about us. The new wonder twins of Ivy Street.

Shivering, I rolled out of bed in slow motion and shrugged into another jumper before climbing back under the covers with my mobile phone. I couldn't seem to get warm. Hearing news of the mayhem that had struck at school hadn't helped me feel any better. What was Eve *up* to?

I switched the tissue to the other nostril and started composing a text message to Jordan Haig. We'd all had his number for ages, someone got it from someone who got it from someone else, and we'd all hugged it to ourselves like a fantasy safety blanket, but no one had ever been brave enough to use it. Until now. The time for helpless drooling was over. He was mixed up in this as much as I was.

So I wrote: *What gives? Storkie*

Resisting the urge to add *x* because what right did I have?

Jordan was a smart guy; his take on things had to be worth at least twice whatever *Today Tonight* had to say about it. Not that I wouldn't be glued to the set by 6.30pm to hear the latest. After a long moment of hesitation, I sent it.

Almost immediately, Jordan replied: *Got my own problems. Her name's Monica but it seems you call her Eve*

Well, that was enough to get me straight out of bed and into my clothes, cold or no cold. Jordan would know what to do. If Eve really was on his case, then he was somehow part of the solution, and it was time to lay a certain ghost to rest.

8

I zipped myself into a mangy velour hoodie and waited. I'd sent him another text, almost immediately, that had said, simply: *I need you to help me end this*

He didn't reply. After an hour, I gave up pacing around my bedroom and headed down to the poky broom cupboard behind the Public Bar that Gran calls 'The Office'. No one would see me in there, least of all Dirty Neil—who'd practically set up house in our fine establishment since I'd been sent home from school, spilling his guts about me to anyone who would buy him a drink. I could pretend to do something useful for Gran while I waited for Jordan to get back to me, if he ever did.

After precisely seventeen minutes of bookkeeping, I

gave up and moped back upstairs to my bedroom to check my mobile. Still no message. So that was it then.

Putting the phone in my pocket, I opened my door to Jordan Haig just standing there, on the threshold. He looked so good. Angry, but good.

Part of me—the mad part—wanted to throw my arms around him the same way I'd done to Floyd Parker. But the rest of me just blushed horribly; hot blood racing up into my neck and my face, beating its familiar path right up into my hairline. I was sure he could feel the heat from where he was standing because he took a step back, like I was a malfunctioning blast furnace.

'How'd y-you get in?' I stammered, shoving loose hair out of my shiny, red-nosed face. In no one's wildest imagination could Jordan be classed as a regular at this pub. If he were, I would only ever leave the premises in cases of dire national emergency.

Jordan just stepped inside and shut the door. I'd like to say I was equally cool. But instead—like some demented game show hostess—I gestured wildly at him to sit down, only to remember that the only place to sit was on my unmade bed and that it was currently festooned in dirty tissues. My inner thermostat kicked up another couple of notches and my skin tone inched towards *magenta crush*.

Wisely, Jordan chose to remain standing. Though what he said next made *me* sit down.

'I just said I was your boyfriend,' he shrugged. 'They let me in, no problems.'

I felt all the blood in my head flow the other way and maybe the room wobbled for a second. If only it were true. That he was here, just for me. I could die then. Die happy.

Ghost, I reminded myself sluggishly. *That's why we're here, remember? Focus.*

Jordan looked like a rock god from head to toe in his bashed-up black leather jacket, worn out tee and denim shirt, skin-tight black jeans and black creepers. He had what looked like two kilograms of silver and onyx strung on narrow leather bands around his wrists. Focus? I could hardly think in a straight line.

I finally croaked, 'She always comes to me at night, Eve. She makes me do things.' My voice sounded like it belonged to someone else who was standing really, really far away. 'How am I able to see her? How is it you can see her, too, when no one else can?'

Jordan shrugged. 'Been asking myself the same questions. No answers presenting themselves.'

He glanced around my room, taking in every dog-eared band poster and unwashed pair of undies lying on the floor before returning his cool gaze to me. 'Maybe it's extra muscle she needs,' he said. 'Or you're not doing the job properly and she's decided to call in a professional.' His laugh was like a bark. 'She's showing me this city place. Some kind of bar.

Wants *me* to go there. She's quite…insistent.'

I felt strangely hurt that Eve had somehow traded up. I mean, I would, if it was a choice between me and him, but it still rankled. 'It can never wait you know,' I heard myself say in that thin, unhappy stranger's voice, not sure why he'd come all this way to tell me himself personally. 'Better hop to it.'

'So I understand,' Jordan replied, mouth curving up into a half-smile that momentarily banished the anger in his eyes. 'But since I've inherited your little problem and I need filling in, you wanna…go see? Car's downstairs.'

I couldn't help the stupid leap of hope in my chest. One day, one day when I was cool, or old, or a hundred times better and more different than I was now, I'd look back on this moment of wild and impossible hope, and throw my head back and laugh. It represented an extra—what— hour in his company, tops? But Jordan Haig and I had to be somewhere *together*, today. I looked down sharply to hide the irrational surge of joy I was feeling.

'Coolio,' I mumbled finally. 'Lead the way.'

As I was scrambling to my feet, Gran suddenly barged in like a pocket whirlwind. She swelled up to almost twice her size when she saw Jordan standing over me, not bothering to wait for an introduction, or an explanation.

'*Who are you?*' she screeched in his face. 'She doesn't *have* a boyfriend.'

Without pausing to breathe, Gran rounded on me next, going a hundred miles an hour like she does when she's stressed. 'What does he want? An exclusive? A photo? Did he hurt you? You invite him?'

My face changed colour a million times then settled on just plain mottled. I felt about two years old, even though I've been able to rest both my elbows comfortably on the top of Gran's head since like, uh, 2012.

'Gran,' I mumbled. 'This is Jordan Haig, a…a guy from my year. We're just going out…for a while.'

The words *for a while* came out sounding funny because the sudden look of hope on Gran's face before she quickly swallowed it down was painful to see. She'd looked the way I was feeling. I'd have to have a quiet talk with her later, let her down gently.

But Jordan didn't help things by saying, 'Being away from Soph, not being able to see her…has almost killed me, Mrs Teague.'

I think Gran's breath caught in her throat the same instant mine did. It wasn't what he'd just said, which my short-term auditory memory was having trouble processing because it was the smoothest-sounding lie I'd ever heard. It was that he hadn't called me *Storkie* or *Stork* the way everyone else did around Gran when they were asking for me. He'd called me by my real name. I didn't think he'd even known it.

He *was* good. So good, I almost believed him.

'It's an honour, Mrs Teague,' Jordan added, politely sticking out his right hand, silver jangling. 'I've been asking to meet you, but you know how she is.' He rolled his eyes.

Gran grasped Jordan's hand, glaring up into his face as they shook firmly. As she looked him over, her expression softened. I could tell she liked him, even though her gaze narrowed momentarily when she clocked the edge of the thin, dark tattoo winding around his right wrist, still visible under all the leather and silver and stone.

But Dad had had one himself. A big Asian dragon with claws and bulging eyes that had worked its way down between his shoulder blades and seemed to blur at the edges, fading as he grew older. The Teagues were no strangers to tattooed men.

'Well, Soph,' Gran said, too cheerfully and loudly after a moment in which I caught her remembering, too, 'you might finally have found yourself a keeper. Enjoy yourselves, darlings, you deserve a bit of time out.'

She ushered us protectively down the back stairs and through the kitchen past Cook before I'd even realised I was moving. At the fire exit, she pushed down on the panic bar securing the fire exit from the inside and propped the door open with her hip.

For a moment, she just stared up at me, looking like she wanted to say something. Instead, she reached up and pushed my impossible hair back from my forehead then hastily swatted Jordan and me out onto the garbage-slick bluestone cobbles of Sancerre Lane before Jordan could change his mind about taking me out.

As she slammed the fire door shut, I could hear her bellowing at someone to *Get the bleeding hell in line*. All class, all the time; that was my Gran.

'Your Gran treat all your boyfriends this way?' Jordan asked, amusement in his deep voice.

My face burned as he pointed in the direction of an old blue Commodore parked fifty metres away, its faded paintwork riddled with rust, a P-plate jammed into the lower corner of the rear window.

Jordan moved before I did, walking towards the front passenger door and holding it open, one dark eyebrow cocked in my direction. Shivering, I pulled the zip of my hoodie higher, the icy wind making my already scarlet nose run again. As I slid into the seat and dabbed self-consciously at my nose with the back of one hand, Jordan slammed the heavy car door shut and went around to the driver's side.

He jumped in behind the wheel and the cuff of his shirt slipped back for a moment. Something weird happened again in the vicinity of my heart, like it was falling from a great height. I could see the word *jymaux* engraved in black upon his skin in tiny letters. It formed part of the dark rim of the tattoo winding around the outer edge of Jordan's wrist. When he caught me staring, he tugged the cuff back up and fired up the engine.

'It means *twin* in Norman French,' he said curtly as he steered up Sancerre Lane and into the stretch of Sancerre Street just outside Floyd Parker's house.

Right-o. I sank down in my seat to avoid any telephoto lenses trained on the area while Jordan turned the corner and began telling me about what I'd missed at school. I closed my eyes, just listening and pretending I hadn't heard it all already from Biddy Cole.

God, he and I are breathing the same air.

Jordan was so *close*. If I put my hand out, I could rest it on his shoulder. It was unreal.

My destructive train of thought screeched to a halt when Jordan added, 'So that's when I worked out my theory about you. You're kind-hearted to a fault. You let people walk all over you, all the time. And you never speak up for yourself, which is perfect for someone like Eve. She's incredibly strong-willed. She must have been interesting to know when she was…'

He hesitated, and the knuckles of his hands went white on the steering wheel, sunlight glinting off the silver around his wrist.

'Alive,' I interrupted gently. 'Say it, Jordan. When she was *alive*.'

9

I told him the two things I knew about Eve: that she was somehow the spit of my own mum and that her biker boyfriend had tried to gun her down in a city street, taking out innocent people instead.

'After that, she disappeared, he disappeared, the news story said. And then about a fortnight later, she shows up at my place and keeps showing up until I do what she wants.'

Jordan was silent for a long time. Though as he eased the car into the bumper-to-bumper traffic on Brunswick Street, he said abruptly, 'I can say this stuff to you, right? Because you're okay.'

Since, like, when? I almost blurted. I had to bite down on the insides of my mouth to stop the words tumbling out.

His grey eyes found mine for a moment before he looked away. 'Even Hendo and Seamus don't know,' he murmured, pushing a fall of dark hair off his face. 'It's not something you want to…advertise.'

I stiffened in surprise. Hendo and Seamus were Jordan's too-cool-for-school wingmen. Jordan had a secret too big even for the both of them?

I found myself holding my breath so hard that purple spots and squiggles started dancing in front of my eyes. Who knew that getting to the bottom of the mystery of Eve would involve seeing inside Jordan's head, too?

He said, in a rush, 'Mum gets impressions, inconclusiveness. She has to work out what they want from the context.'

He swung the car into a narrow side street on the fringes of the city. Old pairs of sneakers hung by their knotted-up laces from overhead wiring like bunches of dingy fruit.

'Mum's…*clairaudient*,' he added hesitantly, like I knew what that meant without a dictionary handy, 'but that's about the extent of it. She hears things, you know?'

I shook my head, still baffled.

'Voices. She says, I'm more…"gifted". I've always been able to see, hear, *smell*. God, how weird does that sound?'

He glanced across at me and I knew I was supposed to react, but it felt like I was hearing him through a heavy veil. None of what he was trying to tell me was really coming together.

'So what I think is Eve—uh, Monica—used *you* to get through to *me*. It's the only explanation. I mean, you're not one of *us*, are you? The people who "see" dead people. And the rest.' He sounded faintly disgusted.

I opened my mouth to tell him about the glowing man from when I was five then shut it again with a snap. I didn't *want* to be one of those people. After Eve, I wasn't going to be one of those people ever again.

Jordan swerved around a cyclist going the wrong way up our street.

'I *hate* it,' he growled, staring sightlessly at the pollution-stained façades sliding by, the cracked and uneven sidewalks. 'I wish they'd leave me alone.' He shot me a sideways look. 'Like how she smells of violets?' he said fiercely, scrubbing at his left arm through the leather of his jacket. 'You get that, right?'

I nodded in confusion: so it was *violets*? I hadn't known that. I just knew I'd never be rushing out and buying any perfume remotely like it. In fact, Eve had just about put me off floral fragrances for life.

'I get that, too,' Jordan growled again, still kneading his left arm before moving on to his right. 'But I can hear her through her memories; feel her. See things she wants me to see. Just snatches. And then there's the rest of them, all talking away like I'm supposed to care. Dropping in and out like crossed wires on a bad line. You can do some of that as well, yeah?'

'Only with *her*,' I exclaimed, mentally crossing my fingers at the lie. 'With Eve. And I can't actually *hear* her, so half of it has been lucky guesses, lucky breaks! I don't get that at all with, uh, others. God, Eve alone is enough to drive anyone mental.'

My voice faltered to a stop as I realised what I was saying and who I was saying it to.

'Yeah,' Jordan looked away, frowning. 'Mental.'

'I didn't mean that,' I responded quickly, waving my hands in the air. 'I'm not sure what I mean. *This* is mental. But you're not. Mental, I mean.'

Oh, honestly, just kill me now, my inner voice moaned as I wailed out loud, 'I always say the wrong thing!'

'See? *See?*' Jordan growled. 'This is what you do. All the time.'

Flushing, I saw that we'd entered the city. Abruptly, he pulled into a *No Standing* zone facing onto a string of eateries that formed the heart of the city's famed Greek quarter. I looked through the window at the fake stalactites hanging from the ceiling inside the souvlaki joint on the corner. I'd never been brave enough to go in. Ever.

'Well.' My voice was tentative. 'It explains how you found me in the middle of a Claudia-and-pals human sandwich. And it explains the total locker meltdown. Eve must have *hated* being ignored by you.'

Jordan replied sharply. 'It stops here. After this, *you leave her alone.*'

I glanced across at Jordan in confusion. He'd ceased worrying away at the skin of his arms. His eyes were closed. He might have been asleep except that the lines of his pale face were tight. My own uneasiness skyrocketed when I realised he wasn't talking to me.

He opened his grey eyes; pupils dilated wide with… pain? Although he was facing me, his gaze was weirdly unfocused, giving the impression he was looking at something else entirely. A chill raced across my skin, making me fold myself down smaller in my seat.

Jordan pointed down the mouth of a narrow city lane just outside my window, lined with Victorian-era warehouses and the back entrances of two-storey shop fronts and fast-food outlets. A delivery truck blocked off the far end of the cobbled lane, offloading steel kegs of beer outside the cellar door of a grim-looking pub with barred windows. If I never saw another beer truck in my life, it would be too soon.

So far, so Melbourne.

'This is it?' I murmured, still confused. 'This is what Eve wanted you to see? So I'm seeing it, and it's not so, um, bad.'

I popped a menthol cough lolly, my nose now so blocked I could barely taste it.

Jordan seemed to snap out of his trance at my words. He nodded, scrambling out of his seat and slamming his car door before yanking mine open.

I climbed out in a tangle of arms and legs, feeling clumsy just because his eyes were on me. An acid spurt of adrenaline flashed through my system as I fished a loose hairband out of my pocket and slung the mess on my head into a low, bushy ponytail.

Not sure what to do with my hands after that, I shoved them both deep into the kangaroo pockets of my hoodie and gave a giant, unlovely sniff. Jordan nearly sent me into cardiac arrest when he hooked his arm through mine.

'Seeing as how I'm supposed to be your boyfriend...' he said, and a ghostly smile flitted across his face.

We entered the laneway. Just being this close to him seemed to pull the world into sharper focus. The layers of graffiti and peeling-away pub-rock posters festooning the walls were suddenly beautiful with colour and texture, and the puddles of filthy water between the cobbles from the overnight rains held a strange surface gleam. A trio of dark-haired cooks in navy aprons on a mid-afternoon smoke-o stared hard at us as we passed by, and I swear I could make out every hair on their unshaven faces as my heart beat hard in my chest.

It's just nerves you're feeling, Stork, I chided myself as Jordan pulled us to a stop a few doors down from where the men still lounged, wreathed in smoke, watching us.

I looked up at the piss-yellow brick façade of a two-storey warehouse, the air dense with the smell of fat frying. There were very few windows, and each was set high up off the ground and plugged by a rectangular pane of greasy, opaque glass, with iron bars from top to bottom. The place had the ambience of a maximum-security jail and the grey metal swing door set at ground level boasted a large sign that read, simply: *Adult Discounters.*

My face flamed as the meaning of the sign soaked in, and I tried to pull away. Even my wildest dreams about Jordan Haig had not featured us walking hand-in-hand through a place that sold plastic sex toys and porno.

'Uh,' I began, and Jordan snorted at my panicked expression, tightening his hold on me as his gaze ran upward. There was a second, smaller sign above the door that bore the legend: *Maximus Lounge.* At night it would light up in neon, but now it was just a bunch of almost burnt-out tubes forming vague letter shapes.

'Two choices,' Jordan murmured, almost to himself. 'What's it gonna be?'

I was seeing oiled men in leather thongs. And not of the footwear variety.

'Uh,' I said again. 'I think Eve meant for me to sit this

one out. She didn't appear to *me*, buddy, she appeared to *you*. She doesn't need me anymore. Your word against mine that I'm even supposed to be here. So you do it. You go and flail through the afterglow of Eve's life, trying to work out what she wants. I've seen enough to last me. Really, I'm good. Happy to pass the baton.'

I tried to disengage my arm once more, but again, weirdly, Jordan resisted.

Then he laughed, suddenly releasing me, and the world was at once colder and dirtier without the warmth of him pressed close. I crossed my arms defensively, but Jordan kept the shocks coming by cupping my face in his hands.

'It's like a game with this one.' His gaze was intent, all trace of amusement gone. 'She doesn't talk to me directly like the others do, she only *shows* me things, things she remembers. And I only hear what she heard, or what she said. She only shows herself to me when I'm with you, did you know that? She only lets me see her when *you're* there. That's never happened before: being able to share this with anyone. Other than my mother.'

His mouth twisted wryly.

'Oh, and the time just after I started primary school. When word got out the little kid in 1F could speak with dead people, everyone was screaming for psych testing. I changed schools a lot before I learnt to keep my mouth shut. So you can see how this is as weird for me as it must be for you. I expected you to run a mile when you found out. But I'm glad you're still here. Surprised. But glad.'

Jordan leaned in abruptly, resting his forehead against mine, and my unreliable breathing cut out altogether as he looked down into my eyes, the two of us forming the apex of something. Some new thing I was too afraid to name for fear it would vanish like star dust.

'She wants you involved, for some reason,' he murmured. 'And I *need* you: to keep me sane. To separate what's *me* from everything else. The usual mechanisms I have for shutting things out—they don't work with her. She found out what my weakness was. She's like a storm front. And because I can't see her when I'm not with you, it feels like it's happening to me, all the little things she feeds me, expecting me to make sense of them. There's no order and no distance: it's like her footsteps are mine, her breathing, her impressions. The fear...'

He swallowed audibly and all my self-consciousness suddenly drained away. Jordan Haig was actually *afraid*. He was more rattled than I, or anyone, had ever seen him. I'd crossed over into scaredy-pants land more times than I could count lately, and a feeling almost of protectiveness kicked in.

I wanted to throw my arms around him again. But it wasn't something I could take back later so, like a coward, I didn't.

'I know it's selfish,' he whispered, 'but you're my control. Come with me?'

'And if she gets what she wants, she'll go away?' I breathed, both wanting it to be true, and not.

'And we go back to being nothing?' Jordan pulled back, his hands falling away as he shrugged. 'Being *normal*? Sure, we can only hope, right?'

He wasn't angry any more, I could tell from his crooked smile. It felt strange, but not uncomfortable, standing here with him, on the verge of leaving sense and logic behind again. There was no one I'd rather be doing this with, I realised.

I took a shaky breath, finally, and nodded. Jordan pulled the heavy door open and held it for me.

I stepped inside and stumbled to a stop only partway in, my eyes struggling to adjust. It was pitch dark in the lobby save for a patch of fluorescent light coming through the glassed-in doorway of the adult shop down a narrow hallway to the right.

I felt around with outstretched fingers in the darkness, like a blind person. Jordan grabbed hold of my left hand as if it was the most natural thing in the world and led me closer to the only light source. As we tentatively shuffled across the uneven, linoleum-tiled floor, hands still linked, I recognised the delicate compound odour of beer, cigarettes and old vomit, a persistent base note of sticky carpet. We were passing a staircase to our left. It had to lead to the *Maximus Lounge*, which would be shut at this hour. There wasn't a sound coming from up above.

We drew closer to the adult store, hands still linked. Through the glass, I could make out an overweight, balding guy in a black tee with a dirty grey ponytail. He was seated behind a counter festooned with penis-shaped party trinkets. He was side-on to us, his eyes glued to an afternoon talk show on an overhead TV. Any moment now, he would turn and see the two of us just hovering by the door like a pair of underage, sex-mad desperados.

I caught a glimpse of boxed-up sex swings, nurses' uniforms and coordinating whip, cuff and chain sets in his or hers colours, fluffy slippers and baby outfits that ran to XXXXL.

'Doesn't do it for me.' I could hear the giant grin in Jordan's voice. He was standing so close I could smell his aftershave, something clean and green-smelling.

I grinned back, on the point of making some lame joke about how we were taking things *way* too fast, when I felt someone brush past me, hard. There was the distinct impression of hip, leg, and denim, so real that I stumbled, turning my head in outrage, exclaiming: 'Hey!'

'What?' Jordan said, puzzled.

He followed the direction of my gaze. Now that my

eyes had adjusted, I could clearly make out the staircase to the lounge running upwards in the fuzzy blackness. That's when it hit me that no one could have come past us, bumping me so hard I'd almost lost my balance. The door to the discounters hadn't even opened to let anyone in or out. The fat guy behind the counter was still glued to the screen.

I felt Jordan tense at the exact same moment I did, the two of us physically recoiling from a roiling wave of crushed violets in the air. It seemed to enfold us like a blanket, thick and overwhelming in the stuffy, claustrophobic dark. I began to cough.

As I watched, eyes watering, the absence of light at the top of the stairs began to silver, faint motes of luminescence gathering to rearrange themselves into a familiar outline: long unbound hair, garb as black as a Greek tragedy, long, bare arms and feet. She was dark energy momentarily corralled into human form, and somehow I knew that the testing was over, that whatever this was that Jordan and I were doing, we were already deep into play. This was the main game, and Eve was in control.

She looked like a queen. She looked like Death itself.

Against inclination, Jordan and I edged closer to her shining form. She was directly above us, at the top of the stairs, and I could feel how every fibre of his being wanted to bolt in the other direction the same way he could feel it in me. We clutched each other close as Eve gazed down at us with her dark, hollow eyes.

'What does she *want*?' I heard myself asking hoarsely, as if I was standing somewhere outside my own body. The things she wanted, expected, were getting worse, I just knew it.

From above, Eve's gaze was unwavering. God, I'd felt her actually *touch* me. Maybe whatever Jordan had, it was catching, and that terrified me even more than seeing Eve again. What had I done? When Jordan had come into the picture, some part of me had hoped that she and I were done for good and everything that had happened was some mere temporary madness, a passing dream.

'Ask her. *Please*.' My voice sounded so remote, faint with dread. I'd started something I couldn't put a name to. I just knew.

Jordan was silent for ages, lost in his peculiar brand of black magic, that queer ability of his to sift through the fractured language of the dead and wrestle sense from it. Though I had my arms around him, he was both there and not there. I wondered what he saw.

Suddenly, he made a choking sound and rocked back on his heels, as if someone had just reached out and punched him, hard, in the throat. He let go of me, gasping, and I braced myself as he swallowed again, the sound so terribly loud in the deserted lobby.

His eyes were wide as he turned to me. 'What she wants,' he gasped, scrubbing at his left arm through the sleeve of his jacket in the way I was beginning to recognise as Jordan-in-distress, 'is, is...'

It was my turn to place my hands on either side of his face. He was breathing hard, like he was trying to outrun something.

'What?' I urged gently, though I couldn't stop the involuntary tremors moving beneath my own skin.

'What she wants,' he tried again, 'is for us to...gather up...gather up...'

I felt my brow wrinkle. *'Gather up?'*

He started to shake again beneath my hands. *'What's left.* She wants us to gather up what remains.'

10

I broke into a cold sweat. And Eve vanished in a gust so strong I felt it lift the ends of my hair. The stairwell went dark. All that lingered was the scent of crushed violets.

I pretty much tried to crawl inside Jordan's jacket at that point, and I noticed he wasn't pushing me away.

'Gather what?' I squeaked. 'Like…body parts?' I craned my head up at the darkness beyond the landing. 'She up there?'

I imagined Eve, slowly disintegrating on beer-stained carpet, in place of the cat lady. And almost gagged as the stench of *Hatherlea* rose up again, ghostly, in my nostrils. If Eve was really up there, it would be cat lady to the nth power.

'I don't know,' Jordan murmured, troubled. 'But there are maybe things she, uh, left behind? I think she wants us to retrieve some…stuff for her. From that bar upstairs.'

'What stuff?' I almost howled. 'What could she possibly want *stuff* for?' I fought Jordan as he started moving towards the stairs. 'She doesn't have any arms or legs, hands. A *head*.'

I struggled in his arms. 'We were only supposed to look,' I insisted, panicked, 'not "retrieve". Retrieval indicates *the further adventures of* and I am *not* in favour. We did what we said we'd do. We came, we saw. Let's call the cops now. They can do the gathering.'

Jordan shook his head. 'No cops. Not if you don't want to be the lead story on *Today Tonight* again. And what would we tell the police? Think about it, Soph.'

It didn't stop me trying to fumble my phone out of my pocket. Jordan wrestled me for it, finally wrapping me in his arms and pinning me so tightly I could barely breathe.

'We can't just walk away,' he insisted. 'She can't do what she needs to do without you. We've let her in, now we have to finish what *you* started. That's how it works or they don't leave, they don't go. You get out of the shower, and someone's standing behind you in the mirror. Every corner you turn, they're just there, waiting and expectant. Piling on the shocks until you give in, or break. It's worse than a horror movie if they don't get what they want. I told you—that's why you don't let them in, *ever*. No undertakings, no little kindnesses, not for the dead.'

Undertakings and kindnesses. Is that what Eve had me engaged in? Whatever the compact was that one made to bind themselves to the dead, I'd done it—in spades.

I was almost sobbing. 'I didn't know! How could I know? I'm not like you, *I've done enough*. I just want her to go away. Make her go, Jordan. You can talk to her. *Make her go*.'

He grasped me by the shoulders. 'I've seen you.' His voice was low and soothing as I hyperventilated so badly that the thick dark began filling up with buzzing pinpoints of light. 'You're nice to everybody. You help everyone who asks you for help, and you don't judge. Do you know how different that makes you from every other freak at Ivy Street?'

'It makes me the freaking freak-of-freaks!'

I struggled harder, trying to block him out. Damn his persuasive hotness, that pine-clean scent of him.

Jordan still held me and shook me gently.

'It's up to us, Soph: you and me. God knows why, but she chose *us*. Could you imagine if Eve had landed on Claudia Perretti's life like a bomb?'

I went still in his arms and the fuzzies began to recede a little. 'I'm not especially *brave*,' I muttered. 'She could at least have factored that into the selection process.'

Jordan ignored me. 'Claudia and her clowns,' he reminded me harshly, 'would have stood by and *watched* as that kid got abducted, or that old guy got run over, or that old woman got eaten alive by her own pets, if they even got to them at all. Most people would. Remember what Mr Connelly said in Legal Studies?'

I looked at him blankly.

'*No duty to rescue*,' Jordan continued. 'So people don't; they don't do anything. They stand back and watch. I'm guilty of that, too.'

'I don't believe you,' I said, shocked that he'd somehow taken notice of every crappy lead feature *Today Tonight* had ever run about me. In order.

'Claudia, Sharys and Harmony wouldn't have lifted a finger,' Jordan insisted. 'They would have said: *Not me, not my problem*. Eve went to the right person for help. Whatever she was before, whatever she is now, she isn't purely destructive. She's just trapped like an animal, and you'd help an animal who was hurt. I know you would.'

'Dogs scare me and I'm allergic to bird feathers,' I said stupidly, before I could stop myself, because self-sabotage comes as naturally to me as breathing.

Jordan's laughter was warm as he released his grip on my shoulders. 'I'm only here because you are. And we will bloody finish this, because I want her off my back. For good. I don't like being told what to do…'

'Or who to do it with?' I snapped back, suddenly hurt. 'It wasn't like I asked for this either. This isn't how I usually go about meeting guys, okay?'

Hot with humiliation, I stumbled forward in the darkness, wanting to get this over and done with, crying out when the toe of my trainer hit the edge of the bottommost stair.

Jordan caught me around the waist as I started to fall and I turned on him. 'So why are we still standing here then? *It can never wait.* Even someone as dumb as I am gets that. Let go of me.'

'Soph,' he began again, but I wrenched out of his grip and lurched up the stairs, patting at the maddening darkness until I found a worn railing running just below waist height up the wall.

'She could have left a light on,' I muttered as the filthy carpet sucked at the soles of my trainers.

I felt Jordan pass me in the dark on the right, taking the stairs easily two, maybe three, at a time. His voice floated down to me from the landing a moment later, so quiet I had to strain to make out his words.

'If she didn't, looks like somebody else did.'

He reached out for me unerringly, guiding me up the last couple of treads.

'Look,' he whispered, his breath warm against my ear. 'There.'

I peered down another murky hall, feeling a slight draft, just a shiver of air against my face, and finally made out a thin line of faint luminescence in the distance. A floor-level sliver of electric light to cut the dark in two.

Jordan tightened his grip on my hand. 'How bad could it be?' he murmured as we padded cautiously down the upper hallway, finding ourselves before a wooden, panelled door.

He didn't hesitate. Before I could catch my breath, Jordan let go of my hand, bracing his shoulder against the door, pushing the heavy thing open with a grunt.

Somewhere deep inside the place, a buzzer sounded twice, faintly. But all we could see, as we entered the Maximus Lounge, was a big, dim, windowless space cluttered almost to the margins of the room with haphazard table and chair arrangements, packed in tight. The air smelt stale—greasy bar snacks cut through with the sour tang of human sweat—and a long, dark wood bar ran along the left hand side of the room, illuminated solely by the light of a single old-style banker's lamp with a green glass shade. Rows of bottles, glasses and silver shakers were silhouetted against a faceted mirror wall. Jordan and I were dimly reflected in it, just a couple of warped, dark shapes in a sea of other ones. Overhead, a fan churned the air lazily, lifting the loose curls on either side of my face. There wasn't another living soul in the rectangular room.

'See if you can find a light switch,' Jordan rasped.

I almost leapt out of my skin when stage lights suddenly went up across the room, centred on a narrow, wooden catwalk, painted a glossy reflective black.

'Is that a, uh, stripper's pole?' I flushed, staring at the end of the projected stage. Mum had described them, but I'd never seen one for real. The glittering thing reached right up into the water-stained ceiling, anchored by two sets of heavy-duty brackets at each end. Two more sets of stage lights flashed on and two more poles were instantly illuminated, one on either side of the catwalk. The backdrop was a swagged dark-red velvet curtain.

A woman dressed entirely in black suddenly emerged from a door hidden somewhere behind it.

For a gut-clenching moment, I thought it was Eve, and I let out a high and breathless scream. Same pale skin and oval face. Same long dark hair hanging loose and forward over her shoulders, that busty hourglass figure.

But the figure shielded her eyes with one hand, barking in a voice that rebounded throughout the cavernous room, 'We're closed.'

Not Eve then. Pissed off, too. I shut my mouth, deeply regretting screaming.

'Monica sent us,' Jordan called out gamely. 'She wants what she left behind.'

The woman froze, one hand raised to shoo us out.

Jordan didn't look at me. Instead, the untouchably cool expression he always sported when Dr Southey tried to throw him a vicious curve ball in Biology slid into place. There hadn't been a trace of doubt in his voice even though I knew that, just under the skin, he was all nerves, like I was.

The woman seemed to give herself a shake before moving down the catwalk hesitantly. 'Monica?' she said bewildered. 'Monica wouldn't send *you*.'

She stopped at the edge of the raised platform and frowned at us through the glare of the footlights. 'You're just kids. Shouldn't even be in here.'

Jordan started moving across the tiled floor, my hand somehow trapped in his again. We made our way through the untidy nests of tables and chairs towards the spot-lit woman, stopping just below her and gazing up.

At close range, she didn't resemble Eve at all. She had deep-set hazel eyes, flecked with pinpoints of deep claret. And it was clear her raven tresses had come out of a Clairol bottle. She was smaller in stature, more fine-boned than Eve. Her tight-fitting, low cut maxi dress was almost too big for her frame, the ends of it dragging on the floor behind her like a Goth wedding train.

The woman's pretty, weary face was alight with fear and hope. But she said again, 'You shouldn't be in here.'

She glanced back at the curtain behind her, adding, 'Cops see you, they could ping us just for you being here.'

'We'll go as soon as we get what Monica sent us for,' Jordan said confidently.

The woman flapped her hands in his face before bunching up her dress in one hand and climbing down off the podium in her teetering heels. She looked up into my face, then Jordan's, searchingly.

'How do I know O'Loughlin didn't send you?' she said. 'Everyone knows he's looking for her. He even came in here, asking. Even after what he did.'

I had to steel my face against wobbling in confusion and giving Jordan away.

'You don't,' Jordan said quietly, his gaze never leaving hers. 'But Monica's somewhere no one can touch her now. That's why she's asking. There's something she needs to do.'

The woman's shoulders visibly slumped in relief until a voice, from behind the curtain, roared: 'Nadja! *I told you to get rid of them.*'

'Got it, Roman, okay?' she bellowed back, though her hands shook as she raked her jet-black curtain of hair back off her face. 'Follow me,' she said quickly, weaving across the room towards the bar.

Jordan and I hovered by the row of fixed, vinyl-topped red stools by the bar while she dug around on the other side of the counter. I could hear doors rapidly opening and closing as she shoved things around, almost talking to herself.

'Doesn't tell me where she's gone, doesn't send texts, emails, nothing, then, like, weeks later she gets youse two to pick up her shit?' Nadja's voice was disgusted. '*That* I believe. Mon all over. Selfish as.'

'Nadja!'

I jumped, glancing back across the room to see a man in charcoal suit trousers and a black, open-necked shirt standing on the platform. He had thick, curling, Italian-Stallion hair cut short and the kind of even tan I'm genetically incapable of reproducing. Somewhere in his thirties, I'd say, with every muscular inch of him screaming: *lifts weights regularly.* And: *thug.* Gran and I knew the type, and they didn't frequent The Star unless things were desperate.

Beneath the harsh lighting the man's black eyes glittered. 'Who *are* you people?' he shouted, jumping down off the stage, striding towards us.

Nadja sprang up above the level of the countertop like a Jack-in-the-box and hastily shoved a bundled-up plastic bag into Jordan's hands across the bar.

'This was hers, this was all,' she gabbled. 'Now get out of here, okay? O'Loughlin's a murderous prick, but he's got nothing on Roman when he's angry. Don't come back. I mean it. And tell her as well. I can't protect her. She's not welcome. Pissed off a lot of people, vanishing like that.'

Jordan nodded his thanks, bundling the green plastic bag and me under his arm. But then he hesitated for a moment and said, 'Nadja? For what it's worth, Monica just wants you to know that she's sorry. She meant to tell you herself before she…left. But she never got the chance.'

'Sorry for what?' Nadja replied, genuine confusion on her pale, pinched face. 'She's got my number. Tell her to use it. Now go. Just *go*.'

Jordan and I spun for the door, but not before Roman's voice sounded out angrily, 'Stop! I said *stop*, you little bastards.'

He crashed into something, swearing and kicking it out of the way as Jordan and I began careening in earnest through the forest of abandoned chairs and tables towards the door.

'Hurry!' Jordan rasped. 'Almost there.'

But I couldn't help looking back over my shoulder. As I watched, Nadja shot out around the front of the bar, moving to head off her boss before he could reach us. My head was pounding. The cold and flu tablets I'd taken this morning had finally worn off. Even the slow stirring of air from the fan was beginning to hurt my skin. I slowed for a moment, clutching at a bentwood chairback, dizzy.

'Soph!' Jordan urged, tugging on my arm.

Behind us, Roman began to shout at Nadja in a language I didn't understand. There was a scuffling sound, a woman's cry, and then Roman was right on top of us, his hand on Jordan's shoulder. As he swung Jordan around, pulling us both off balance, I caught sight of Nadja kneeling on the floor tiles near the bar, her long hair covering her face.

'You little *shits*!' Roman snarled as Jordan pushed me into the space behind him, the door close at my back. 'You don't just walk into my place and take stuff off the premises without consulting with me first.'

Roman snatched the bundle of plastic out from under Jordan's arm, shoving him hard into me for good measure, before digging around in the bag and pulling out a guy-sized black T-shirt with a Death's head design on it, entwined with silver daggers and red roses. Gran and I called the look *gay-designer-pirate*. Everybody who dressed like that drank two doors down, at *Deezy's*.

As the T-shirt slid free of the plastic, a greeting card, a cheap ballpoint pen and a loose blue envelope fluttered to the ground. I bent, intending to retrieve them, but Roman wagged a chunky finger at me.

'Uh uh.' He swept the card up off the ground, frowning over the cartoony *Thank you!* message on the outside, then the words scrawled across the inside in big, loopy handwriting.

Upside down, Jordan and I read:

To Carter K – for services rendered.
Always, M x

'You Carter?' He looked up, addressing Jordan belliger-
ently. 'Lots of people been looking for Monny's little friend.
Didn't think you was real.'

Jordan shook his head. 'Just the courier,' he mumbled.
'Pick up, drop off. Owed someone who owes someone a
favour. Don't know nothing.'

At the periphery of my sight I saw Nadja's head come
up sharply at Jordan's words. Roman's gaze narrowed on
me, mashed into the door by Jordan's weight and barely
breathing.

'I *know* you,' Roman said, frowning, dark eyes raking
my face.

'Don't know you,' I replied, shaking my head, my fat
ponytail bouncing on one shoulder. 'Never been here
before, never seen you before, I swear.'

'But I seen *you*,' Roman said, dropping the card and
T-shirt as he shoved Jordan out of the way. He gave me
a slow top-to-toe once-over that made my skin crawl.
'Yeah. You're that skinny bitch they're calling the
North Fitzroy Nostradamus, *The Saviour of Sancerre
Street*. Say you saved all those people because you can *see
the future*.'

He mimed talking marks in the air, his laughter unamused.

'You got the wrong person,' I whispered.

'She's just my girlfriend,' Jordan interjected, and it sounded so real tripping off his tongue that, even now, I ached for it to be true. 'We're not even here, okay?'

Roman ignored him, placing a hard finger under my chin and lifting it so that I couldn't look away. I had at least a couple of inches on him, but his menacing presence, his virulent cloud of aftershave, seemed to fill my entire world.

'The Reavers like to drink here,' he said slowly and clearly. 'It's almost a home away from home for Keith O'Loughlin and his boys. That's all I'm saying.' He thrust his jaw in Nadja's direction. 'She's his favourite. Likes his women to look like women, look like *her*. The tits, the long black hair. Very particular on that score. Has a type.'

The man's laughter was harsh.

'Take a good look into your future, girly, and you'll see Keith O'Loughlin and his mates standing in it if you're not careful. Everyone knows where you live. All it would take would be one word from me that you were here on Mon's behalf, and you'd be dead. O'Loughlin's not a forgiving man.'

Roman shoved me away so hard the back of my head smashed into the door. Then he turned, on the verge of walking away, when he suddenly spun back around, jabbing his finger into my breast bone. '*Today Tonight*—is that what this is all about? You miked up?'

Deliberately keeping me out of Jordan's reach, Roman put his hands around my waist and I stood very straight in the tight circle of his grip, trying not to shudder.

'Is it?' he murmured, his hands moving up and down my sides, drifting down across my hips and up my spine. He followed the meagre curves of my body in a parody of a shake down, knowing it would revolt me.

I shook my head, feeling hot and sick under his touch, gazing at a point to the left of Roman's head as his hands continued their lazy exploration. 'Mon owes me money, and a lot more besides,' he murmured intimately. 'You see her, you tell her she'd better be ready to pay up.'

'Hey,' Jordan snarled, gripping me by the arm and pulling me back into his body so hard that Roman was forced to let go. 'Hands off, *buddy*. We were just supposed to pick up a bag. That's all. Not cop a free feel.'

Roman leered into both our faces. 'So pick it up then, *buddy*, and piss off. Neither of you got the goods to work here. Get.'

He threw his head back and laughed, striding away in Nadja's direction as I scraped the T-shirt, card and envelope off the ground, stuffing them into the plastic bag with trembling hands.

'Let's go,' I hissed, still feeling the man's hard fingers

on the sides of my breasts. 'Jordan, *please*.'

I bit the insides of my cheeks to hold back my tears as Jordan pulled the door open to let us out. Before it even had time to swing closed on the Maximus Lounge, we were half running, half stumbling down the reeking, silent upper hallway, laughing in sheer terror.

11

When we were both safely inside the car, accelerating away, I started dry heaving in shock, sprawled lengthways against the door. Jordan wisely kept his silence until we reached the outskirts of the city.

'Want me to stop the car, Sophie?' he asked.

But I managed to slide back up into a sitting position and fumbled back into my seat belt.

'I'd just like to go home, please,' I replied, my voice very small. I crossed my arms tightly over my chest. All Roman had done was touch me through my clothes, but I still felt dirty. How had Mum stood it all those years she was a 'dancer'?

I sniffed, blinking back the urge to sneeze and cry at

the same time, and Jordan shot me a white-faced look. The rolled up plastic bag was nestled on his lap like a small, sleeping animal that could turn feral if provoked.

'It's my fault,' he muttered, pushing a fall of brown hair out of his eyes.

I shrugged, trying to show him I was totes cool with hard fondling from a perfect stranger. 'What? That I'm a prude? How could it be?'

Jordan shook his head. 'Once the lights went up, once we knew what that place was, I should have had you wait outside. I should have known.'

'Your expertise extends to reading the dead, not the living,' I said hollowly, 'don't sweat it, mate.'

Jordan renegotiated our original route in reverse, tossing me the plastic bag at one of the intersections. I pulled out the men's T-shirt and held it up for him at the next change of lights.

He wrinkled his nose. 'That's it?' he said. 'That's not an answer, that's a fifteen-dollar shirt.'

'There was that card,' I responded numbly, feeling his disappointment; I felt it, too. Eve—I couldn't bring myself to call her *Monica*—hadn't given us enough to go on.

We were two streets away from The Star. I slumped down lower in my seat in case it was a slow news day and rabid journos were still parked out front. While I was making myself as small as possible, Jordan fished the card out of the plastic bag and rested it on the dashboard, re-reading it out loud.

> *To Carter K – for services rendered.*
> *Always, M x*

'No good,' he muttered as he took the narrow, concealed entrance that fed into Sancerre Lane and the back entrance of The Star. 'Gives us nothing.'

'You're telling me?'

Jordan dug around in the bag some more and retrieved the blue envelope. His expression suddenly changed and he turned the front of it in my direction as he steered the car slowly up the lane.

'Carter Kelly,' I read aloud. It was written in the same loopy hand from the inside of the *Thank You!* card.

Eve had maybe started to write the guy's address on the front. There was a single vertical line under the name. But she'd never gotten any further before she'd shoved the envelope back in the bag.

'How many C. Kelly's could there be in the book?' I said wearily as we bumped down the cobbles towards home past the usual array of locked up, spray-painted garage doors.

'Plenty,' Jordan replied with a frown. 'That's the problem. People called Kelly aren't exactly thin on the ground. You'd have to call each one. And the right guy might not even be listed.'

'I can start looking once I get inside,' I murmured. 'I'll be fine once I get inside. Really, I'll take it from here. I'm used to Eve's, um…'

'*Methodologies*?' Jordan cut in. 'I still don't know how you identified all those people if this is the kind of *help* she gives you. You're amazing, you know that?'

'Like, the opposite of,' I retorted, leaning back against my headrest.

I looked up through the window at a sudden bright break in the clouds, feeling the faint warmth of the late afternoon sun on my face for the first time that day. I closed my eyes momentarily.

'It was all dumb luck, J. The usual way I operate.'

He pulled to a stop outside The Star's fire door. I scraped myself together and undid my seat belt. Everything hurt. To make matters worse, I had to tip my head back at an oblique angle to stop the snot from leaking out my nose in a thin stream.

Jordan leaned back against the driver's door, looked at me. 'I'll just come in, make sure you're okay,' he said in a neutral voice.

Wordlessly, I popped my own door and shouldered it open, almost falling flat on my face on the bluestone cobbles outside.

As Jordan pushed open his door, I held up one hand,

palm out, noticing with a detached, I'm-about-to-burn-all-my-bridges-with-the-hottest-guy-in-school kind of calm, that I was noticeably swaying from side to side like a drunk elephant. The urge to flee was rising in me, like a scream.

'I need a bad-ass dose of antihistamines,' I rasped into his face across the roof of the car, swiping at my nose with the back of my sleeve for that extra touch of elegance. 'What I *don't* need, Jordan Haig,' I added, wagging a shaky finger at him, 'is expectation and hope. I need to get this goddamned phase of my life over with so that my sparkly-arkly future—whatever that is—can start. Now just go home, will you?'

I squinted at my surroundings beadily, imagining a lingering scent of violets wrapping around me in the chill air and swung my pointer finger in a semi-circle.

'All of you. *Go home*. Trouble me no further this night.'

Having delivered possibly the last words I would ever speak in Jordan Haig's hearing, I swerved around the front of the car in the direction of the fire door. But Jordan somehow got there before I did and we stared each other down. The sound of my own blood was roaring in my ears. I had to force myself not to look away first. We were standing so close to each other, I could see every tiny, milk-coffee coloured freckle dappling the bridge of his excellent nose, and I'm sure it was likewise from his POV, except my nose was red.

It was excruciating meeting his eyes but, for once, I refused to back down.

'I am trying to tell you to go away,' I muttered with as much dignity as I could manage. 'I'm trying to tell you that I don't need your help and you aren't reading the signals. Damn it.'

'Actually, I'm not angry anymore,' Jordan replied cheerfully, as if we were having an entirely different conversation. 'Now? I'm kind of enjoying myself.'

Nonplussed, I watched as he banged on the steel fire door with the flat of his free hand like that lie he'd told security was true and he had every right to see me inside.

'You're a funny girl, Soph,' he said. 'Now that you've got my full and undivided attention, shut your mouth and try to look happy. Do you know how many girls would *kill* to be in your position?'

He gave me a sideways shove with one elbow. And then he grinned, just to show he was joking. A wide, sustained, toothy grin that changed all the lines of his angular face completely and crinkled up the skin around his grey eyes.

Something inside me flipped over, pancake-style, even though he was a lost cause. No guy forms lascivious intentions about a girl who screams like, well, a girl and wipes her nose on the back of her hand because she forgot to pack tissues.

So I said, gruffly, to shield myself from the sudden rush of hurt, 'And your opinion means so much. *Now get off me.*'

I shoved Jordan back so hard he fell off the step we were standing on, almost dropping Monica's plastic bag. He started laughing.

There was a muffled clank from the other side, then the heavy steel door creaked open. Eric the dreadlocked dish pig stuck his head out cautiously, doing a triple-take when he saw it was me standing out there. With a guy who appeared to be enjoying my company.

'You look like shit, Soph!' Eric exclaimed when he'd gotten his face back under control. 'And you're supposed to be *inside* the, uh'—he made exaggerated talking marks with his fingers—'*security cordon*. Is that the boyfriend everyone's talking about?'

I glared at Eric so fiercely that he darted aside to let us pass. Still grinning, Jordan guided me down the back hallway past Gran's empty office.

'Walk faster,' I murmured. 'Don't want to be seen. No mood for questions.'

But Gran caught the edge of Jordan's lean denim-clad hip heading up the staircase to my bedroom because Gran never misses a trick.

'Soph?' she called out, peering around the open double doors to the Public Bar. 'Jordan? Is that you?'

Through the doorway behind us, I caught the stares of at least a half-dozen interested parties looking on from behind their beers, their eyes and ears almost hanging out on stalks.

At the mention of Jordan's name, Dirty Neil actually levered his permanent leer and visible span of bum crack off his usual stool and shambled to the door with a half-finished beer in his hand, the better to eyeball us. He took a huge pull of his drink, giving Jordan the evil eye—which was hard, because Jordan had at least ten centimetres on him.

Dirty Neil's voice was surly. 'Where d'you think you're off to, sport? Only bedrooms upstairs.'

'To do some research,' Jordan replied coolly, letting go of me and standing taller.

'I'll bet,' Dirty Neil shot back, his eyes sliding down the length of my shivering, feverish body like a greased spit ball.

I heard Jordan's angry intake of breath and his profile went hard, the tension in the air almost crystallising.

'Gran?' I pleaded, unused to the feeling of being contested territory. The fact that it had happened twice in one day was seriously spinning me out and something in my red-raw face made Gran turn on Dirty Neil immediately and drive him back into the Public Bar with the back of the vinyl-covered menu she was holding in her hand.

'Last time I looked,' I heard her scoff, 'she already had a grandmother and her name's not Neil Douglas, *Neil Douglas*. So get your nose out of Sophie's business and back into the business of drinking your beer. Pour you another?'

Still bristling, Jordan pushed the sleeves of his battered leather jacket right up past his elbows, giving me a full view of the serious work he'd had done to his skin.

Up close, none of the symbols made any kind of sense. They were densely layered and formed patterns that seemed to flow and shift into each other. Here and there I recognised something familiar, like a flower, or a skull, or a boat in full sail, but the rest of it was probably in a language no one alive spoke any more, or maybe ever had; Jordan appeared to have whole phrases written on his skin in a spidery, Gothic script. I'd never been close enough to him to see the stuff he'd had done, but some of it looked pretty insane: fully Death Metal, I'm-a-closest-Satan-worshipper-for-real insane.

He shot me a dark look. 'He always treat you like that? Like you're his personal property?'

I turned, furious at the casual judgment in Jordan's tone. 'He's an amoebic life form compared to that Roman guy, and I can handle it. *Have* been handling it—for a long time. I'm tougher than I look, hotshot.'

But then a wave of pain overcame me and, for a second, I had to look down. 'If Dad were here,' I murmured, 'Neil wouldn't dare. And he knows it.'

'Your dad walk out on you, too?' Jordan asked, a wealth of leashed anger in his voice.

'No, he died,' I mumbled, putting a hand up defensively before Jordan could get a word out. 'And it's okay, now. It's fine.'

Which was the lie it sounded like. Not trusting myself to meet Jordan's eyes, I poked instead at his heavily inked left arm as we mounted the stairs side-by-side. 'So,' I said, taking a deep breath to push down the pain, 'what do all these *mean* then, really?'

Jordan held up the inside of his left forearm to my scrutiny, the light from the jukebox on the landing casting strange shadows that seemed to bring some of the tattoos to life before he lowered his arm.

His reply was matter-of-fact. 'They're extracts from certain *grimoires*.'

'Grim-what?' I muttered as we reached the upper floor. To get to my bedroom and Gran's, which were right at the end of the upstairs corridor, you had to pass a number of suites we maintained for those pub patrons too blotto to make it home at closing time. No one was currently residing *Chez Teague*, so every door was open, each 'suite' looking more wincingly lurid than the last.

We'd passed a couple of rooms when Jordan jammed the plastic bag under one arm and started pressing his fingers into the exposed flesh of his forearms like he was cold.

'*Grimoires*,' he said again distractedly. 'So-called ancient textbooks of magic that have been widely circulating for centuries, some in Old French, some in Latin.'

'Magic?' I exclaimed.

'Just protective magic,' he muttered, 'nothing black. We made sure. At least, Daughtry did.'

'Daughtry?' I said, confused. As far as I knew, no one at Ivy Street answered to that name.

'He's a friend,' Jordan replied carefully. 'Well, of Mum's. Big French guy. Looks like a Viking—wears his hair in a blond plait, with this wooden stick pushed through it, I kid you not. And silver.' Jordan shook his wrists so they jangled. 'He got me onto the silver. Actually,' he added, 'Daughtry kind of scares me.'

'Because he's, like, a magician?' I laughed nervously. 'Seriously?'

'To tell you the truth,' Jordan mused, 'I don't know *what* he is. He's gone for months at a time, then suddenly rings Mum up for a chat over a cuppa. They get on like a house on fire. It's weird. Met at one of those New Age fairs at the Convention Centre where everyone does aura readings and unblocks your chakras for a fee and stuff. He just walked up to her and got talking and they've been friends ever since. When I told Daughtry how much I hated them all coming through, well, he suggested I get these.' Jordan looked down at his forearms and his voice grew hesitant. 'The tatts and stone and silver have kind of…helped.'

'Maybe Daughtry's sweet on your mum?' I said.

Jordan shot me an admonishing look. 'That's *sick*, Soph. He's not much older than we are. But, anyway, he knows things. Wacko stuff that's off-the-map. That sharpened stick he wears in his hair? He says it's some kind of weapon or key. *Yeah, right, mate*, I always tell him. *It's a stick.* But I don't think he's ever been to school…'

Jordan stopped dead without warning at the doorway of an empty room we were passing and I almost ran into the back of him.

'We call it the *Orange Room*,' I said apologetically, as he surveyed the room, 'for reasons that should be blindingly obvious.'

Everything in the room just *was*—even the balding, dip-dyed flokati rug. The centrepiece of the whole visual nightmare was a sagging double bed with a fluffy, razor-cut orange chenille bedspread. The bed was flanked on one side by an orange, vinyl-covered 70s armchair and on the other by a Formica-topped bedside table that had begun life as a hallway telephone stand. The late afternoon sunlight flooding the room made even the dust devils seem orange.

'We like to match,' I muttered faintly, wondering what my life must seem like to him. 'Now hurry up and walk me to my bedroom and *get the hell out of here*, Jordan, so that my reputation as a dork who can't get a date remains intact. You can't be seen with me. This is "Storkie" Teague you're messing with. The person who's so freakishly tall, thin and all-round *stupid*, it defies logic. And I'm quoting here.'

Jordan shot me a quick, closed look that could have meant anything.

'Old head on a stick?' I continued, on a real roll now. 'Butt of all jokes? The boobless wonder who moonlights as a reserve player on the boys' senior basketball team? I'm "the human firelighter", remember? Everyone's mate, nobody's bestie. Storkie, the undateable life form.'

I tried not to sound bitter, but I must have, because Jordan now gave me a sharp, sideways glance before ducking into the orange room.

'If you believe a word of what you just said, then you really *are* stupid,' he muttered, approaching the warped impression in the floorboards at the foot of the bed that had been there for as long as we'd owned the pub. 'This is how it begins,' he then mumbled, and I wasn't sure if he was talking to himself, or to me.

'What begins? Lessons in bad taste?' I replied with a sigh, reluctantly trailing Jordan into the room. I'd never liked this one, and it wasn't just that I clashed horribly with everything in it. Entering it always seemed to make my head hurt. If it ever needed cleaning or tweaking, I'd put it off until Gran rolled her eyes and did it, or got someone else to.

I hadn't been in the room for months, but it struck me suddenly that the warping in the floorboards had gotten a lot worse; it had the profile of a small hillock now, as if the floor was somehow elastic and something pointed was pressing up sharply from underneath. As far as I knew, there was nothing but empty air under that floor. The Sports Bar, with its bank of TV screens fixed 24/7 on the races or the match of the day, ran beneath it.

'Weird, huh?' I said, looking down at the small mound at our feet. I could feel my heartbeat pounding in my temples the way it always did in here.

Jordan poked at it with his creeper-shod foot then sucked in a deep breath as if he'd cut himself.

Something about the repetitive way he kept pressing at the flesh of each arm reminded me of someone playing the keys of a piano.

With a chill flash of insight, I wondered why it had taken me so long to actually *see* what he was doing. Blinking, I remembered the lockers erupting at school; the hail of physical objects that had defied the laws of gravity and barely seemed to touch him as he'd pressed and pressed on his arms.

'You're hitting them in some kind of order,' I whispered,

backing away from him at the realisation. 'Those words and pictures. Aren't you?'

Jordan raised his gaze to mine in misery, then his grey eyes flicked past me, locking onto something—something in the room with us—and he snarled, '*Sunto!*'

12

'Stay away!' Jordan snapped. *'Je suis un mastin.'*

The language he was speaking had a guttural accent, and I can't properly describe what happened next.

It's like…something attached itself to the skin of my *face*.

I brushed it off with a shriek, this thing I couldn't see. It had the feel of cobwebs, but worse. Sentient cobwebs? Spider silk, but with purpose.

Then there was a momentary pressure on my chest, as if someone had laid a heavy stone on me, or maybe the spider silk was somehow burrowing under my skin and heading for my lungs, because for a second I couldn't breathe.

'*Jor-dan*,' I choked out, clawing at the air in his direction. 'Help.'

'*Tradiment!*' Jordan roared, extending his right arm in a sweeping motion that ended at the empty armchair across the room. The plastic bag we'd retrieved from the Maximus Lounge fell to the floor with a rustle.

The pressure just worsened. I shook my head, tears pouring down my face as I struggled for air and Jordan thundered again, still indicating the chair, '*Sunto!*'

The pressure abruptly lifted. But the room now seemed shrouded in shadow, as if the late afternoon sun was fighting its way through some sort of otherworldly filter, or something filmy yet dense was passing before my eyes.

Then I could breathe again, and the lurid brightness of the room was as it always was. Maybe I'd imagined everything.

Jordan glared at the empty chair for a moment, arms crossed over his chest. Then he calmly turned his back on the empty, vinyl-covered seat and pulled me close, resting his chin on my hair as I gulped and shuddered on his shoulder, hands covering my tear-stained face.

'You're safe now,' he rumbled, a hand at the base of my spine, I felt it burning there. 'I'm here.'

'What does it mean? You know, all that *mass-tan* stuff?' I stumbled over the word, still gasping.

Jordan's mouth twisted. 'It's one of Daughtry's sayings.

It's a declaration that's supposed to *contain and compel*. "Mastin" is what he calls people like us. It's Norman French. It means gate keepers, guardians, the ones who stand between *them* and *the great unwary*—as he likes to call most people. Mastin, he says, have the ability to move between this world and *Sheol*.'

He laughed, and I could hear the scepticism in it.

'Sheol?' I croaked, looking up at him.

'The underworld,' Jordan replied in a sepulchral whisper. 'The place things like Eve come from and go to. Though I consider myself more of a low-level watch dog,' he added in a more normal voice, 'prepared to turn a blind eye. Knowledge is a dangerous thing, and I want to sleep at night. Daughtry wants to train me up, teach me what he knows, but I always turn him down.'

Jordan's chuckle was now rueful, like it was some kind of longstanding bone of contention between him and this Daughtry guy.

'One world with *these* things in it?' He indicated the chair in the corner with a tilt of his head. 'Is more than I can stand. I don't need another one. I hope I never see Sheol. If it even exists.'

I ground the heels of my hands into my eyes. '*That* wasn't Eve, was it?'

It had felt different, and I couldn't explain, how I'd known immediately.

Jordan ruffled the ends of my ponytail, trying to keep his voice light. 'No,' he replied. 'It wasn't.'

'Then let's get out of here,' I begged, pulling him out of the room I vowed to never willingly enter again.

Behind me, I heard Jordan hook up the fallen plastic bag before saying, almost apologetically, 'For us, the extracts act as a kind of protective amulet or armour when worn on the skin. If I touch certain symbols, read them in a certain order, I can keep most of it—*them*—out. It has something to do with channelling the memory of intense pain. Daughtry said you weave it about you like a net they can't reach through. Set them from you, set them back, he always says, with natural magic and pain and they will have to abide by your decision *not* to act on their behalf. Your pain will always more than equal theirs because yours exists in the realm of living memory. That is, unless your guard is down—the way mine was, with you.'

'Hey, *hey*,' I said, glancing sharply at him as we stopped short outside my closed bedroom door. 'You can't be blaming *me* for Eve? She's a freaking force of nature. And that "net" of yours didn't keep that *thing* from trying for *me*.'

My hands rose to the base of my throat involuntarily at the memory of fleshless, weightless fingers.

Jordan dropped the plastic bag and grasped my hands,

reeling me in closer to his body. 'What can I say?' His smile was crooked. 'They're opportunistic.'

'Opportunistic?' I wailed, pulling free. 'I wish you hadn't told me. It was better not knowing.'

'See what I mean about knowledge?' Jordan replied. 'But, anyway, he's benign. He just doesn't like the poker machines you've installed in the Sports Bar. The noise… bothers him. And the floor is his way of telling you that. That, and he's not going anywhere any time soon. He likes it here. He died decades ago, right in that very room. But he loved the place so much, he never left.'

I froze in the act of reaching for the door handle. 'He's *dead*, Jordan. He's not supposed to have opinions.'

'The floor's only going to get worse unless you do something,' Jordan added helpfully. 'Just saying.'

I glared at him. 'I can change the fit out of the Sports Bar about as much as I can change my bra size,' I snapped before my brain caught up with my mouth. 'And you bloody well know it. Gran hates the things, but we only just put them in and it's our livelihood we're talking about and *we have to survive somehow.*'

Now I was channelling my own grandmother. Things couldn't get any better.

Jordan's eyes glinted down into mine in amusement as he leant against my bedroom door, his rangy leather-clad torso framed by my rampaging glitter sticker collection. I swore to myself I would remove every stupid, shiny thing before the week was through, even if it meant breaking every one of my fingernails.

The heaviness in my chest returned as Jordan continued to hold my gaze.

'Marshmallows like you don't stand a chance,' he grinned suddenly and it was like a bolt of electricity hearing him refer to me the same way Mum used to.

'So it's lucky you've got me.'

It was so far away from the truth, I looked away, hurt.

'You can go now,' I said, staring at my feet. 'I'll let you know what I find—if and when.'

Jordan lifted my chin so that I was forced to look into his eyes.

'You're doing it again,' he chided, 'and I meant what I said as a compliment. Eve really must have been something when she was alive. She must have been some kind of nuclear-powered bitch who specialised in getting her own way. It still comes through, you know, that *can't-take-no* part of her. To me, they're like…bars on a light spectrum, some are so faded and pale they're easy to ignore. Press the symbols and they're gone, dismissed. But she's fierce, Eve, white-hot. Sometimes, when she's showing me something she thinks I need to see, I forget she isn't a real person anymore. Someone as soft-hearted as you *needs* a watchdog. That's all I'm saying.'

'Can I go now?' I pleaded.

Jordan shocked me by shaking his head.

'She *did* use you to get to me,' he insisted quietly. 'There's always background noise around me, things I see out of the side of my eye that shouldn't be there, odours that persist when they shouldn't, things I know before I should even know about them at all. As soon as I was forced to look at you, really look, I could see her, too. That's what she wanted. But I resisted for as long as I could...'

'Yeah,' I said, miserable, 'because I'm so resistible, I get it. *I get it.*'

Feeling betrayed, I yanked on the door handle, placing my body in the widening gap. 'I'm here now, I'm "safe",' I said, face burning, 'so take your misguided sense of chivalry, Jordan, and go. I'm perfectly capable of finding Carter Kelly on my own. I work better solo. I have *form.*'

I tried to shut the door in his face, a half-sob caught high in my throat, but Jordan's right hand shot out and held me in place.

'*My guard was down,*' he growled, 'because every disembodied spirit from here to Kingdom Come seems to know you're my weak spot, Sophie Teague. I was never going to do anything about it because what would have been the point? My last girlfriend, let's see, two schools back, tried to stage an intervention that involved several extended family members, a lay priest, a large wooden club and rolls and rolls of cling film. I declined to press charges in the end. But there you have it, now you know.'

My mouth was doing that falling-open thing again, until I realised, and shut it with an audible snap of teeth.

'I *want* to be here,' Jordan said. 'I didn't at first, you've got me there, but now I do. I'd resigned myself, don't you see? I didn't see a way to be *like this*'—he gestured roughly at himself—'and still be with somebody else. But now I'm officially un-resigning. *You didn't run away.* That's what Eve saw in you, too. I'm not normal but neither are you! If I had to be stuck working errands for a pushy dead woman, you'd be the one I'd want on my side. You've proven yourself over and over. You're gold. You've been *unreal*, I don't think you realise how much.'

He pulled me into him and I could feel my bedroom door swing open behind me the same way something inside my head seemed to be shifting to let the light in.

'Since you came to Ivy Street you're the first person I look for, every morning, did you know that?' His voice was strangely urgent. 'Even if it's just a glimpse of your bright hair, drifting past. And I always told myself I'd talk to you one day, but then the side of me that believes in sense and logic would talk me right back out of it, because how would it be fair to inflict *me* on someone? It's never going to go away. The weirdness. Not ever. Not until I die. Daughtry says so. You don't choose this, you're born with it and you just learn to…cope. The more you see them, *the more you see them*, Soph. It's not a "gift". It's the worst kind of curse.'

Jordan made a hiccupping sound that I realised was forlorn laughter.

'When I can't cope'—he looked down and flexed his partially inked right arm—'I just get more of these. Soon I'm going to run out of space.'

It was maybe the most Jordan Haig had ever said to me, or anyone, in a single go, in his entire life.

But when I still didn't reply, mainly because I couldn't find any words, he muttered, 'I noticed you the minute you walked into our form room. You were so tall and pale that the sun seemed to be shining *through* you. But you were too busy looking for crumbs of kindness from all those try-hard morons to even make eye-contact and then the pattern was set. It was me and Hendo and Seamus versus everyone else. It's like we're ring-fenced by electricity. Everyone treats us like we're freaks.'

'More like apex predators!' I murmured finally, too dazed to take it all in. 'It's the tatts, Jordan. They give you this untouchable aura…'

Jordan looked down at his bared forearms ruefully. 'Which is only supposed to work against the dead, not the living. And I *like* that you're tall…' he added so quickly that I almost missed the words, '…because it makes it so much easier for when I want to kiss you…'

And then he did, and we staggered backwards through the open door of my bedroom, pressed together, clinging to each other like two drowning people, and it was only the thought of having the most precious moment of my entire life witnessed by some punter who'd missed the turn off to the toilets and kept climbing that made me tear my lips from Jordan's and plunge my scalding face into the side of his neck.

'You taste like a packet of Butter-Menthols,' Jordan murmured into my hair.

'There are at least a dozen semi-legless adults down-stairs,' I whispered, half ecstatic, half terrified, 'and *my gran*, who knows and sees all. We're supposed to be doing *research*, remember?'

Terror and lust warring in me, I reached around him and pushed the door closed, so that only a narrow band of hallway showed through.

Seemingly oblivious to my tissue-infested room, the purple and orange pair of discarded undies on the floor right by his foot, Jordan linked his hands at the small of my back and pulled me close again.

'This *is* research, Soph,' he murmured. 'I'm finding out about you and how you react to me. I've never wanted this gift: I spent my whole life trying to ignore it, keep it hidden. But it brought me *you*. Somehow Eve knew to involve the one person at Ivy Street High that I seriously don't hate being around, who sees me the way I am and isn't…afraid.'

I discreetly nudged the underpants back under the edge of my quilt with the toe of my grubby trainer as he pushed my heavy hair back off my face.

'Doesn't it worry you?' I whispered. 'That she slipped your defences? It worries me lots.'

Jordan laughed. 'Yeah, I lie awake at night wondering what kind of undead Trojan horse I've let in. But what's the worst she can do to us that she hasn't already inflicted on you? The cat lady looked baaad.'

'The cat lady pretty much took the cake,' I agreed, swallowing.

Jordan leant forward and kissed me lightly on the mouth and my cheeks flamed up so brightly it made him laugh.

'See? And you managed that one all on your own. You're the bravest person I know, Soph. And now there are two of us to work out what Eve needs.'

He flicked my cheekbone with one finger and smiled.

'And after she's gone, we'll still be here, trying to figure each other out. So let's get to work and get her the hell out of our lives already, okay? Because we don't need an audience. Not for this.'

It was nearly dinnertime, and the light outside had long since faded to a pink-limned grey.

As I continued to hesitate just inside the door, Jordan strode across my bedroom with a long-limbed grace and threw himself into the creaky captain's chair in front of my open laptop, powering it up before peeling off his leather jacket and slinging it over the curved chair back. He clicked on my sticker-covered desk lamp and rolled up the unbuttoned sleeves on his denim shirt, querying, 'Password?' as if he hadn't just been kissing me breathless moments before.

I perched on the edge of my battered desk, shielding the screen with the curve of my body as I quickly typed in my password and brought up the residential directory for the state.

There was a surname box, and I typed in: *Kelly*. In the blinking box beside it I typed: *Carter*.

Nothing came up.

So I cut the word 'Carter' down to a 'C' and, literally, one hundred and one hits came up, citing addresses everywhere from *Spotswood* to *Bonbeach* and places I'd never heard of before that sounded far away and impossible to get to like *Kurunjang* and *Barnawartha*.

'This is hopeless,' I blurted out, as Jordan scrolled down the long list of names. 'We can't call them all and ask if they take a size "M" in men's tees and, by the way, do you know an insistent, deceased woman called Monica?'

'Let's try a slightly different angle,' Jordan murmured, nudging me aside. 'What was that guy's name again? The shooter?'

I watched, stunned, as Jordan typed in, *O'Loughlin, K.* Name and address details popped up obligingly. 'Just seven,' Jordan said with satisfaction.

'*You're not serious?*' I exclaimed. 'The guy's supposed to be a psychopath. You can't just call a psychopath asking for answers!'

Jordan dug around inside his leather jacket and pulled out his mobile phone. 'Why not? What are the chances any of these people have Caller ID?' he said, already dialling.

'He *killed* someone, Jordan!' I squeaked, aghast, as Jordan said, 'Oh, good afternoon, I was wondering if I could speak with Keith O'Loughlin?'

'That's right, *Keith*.' There was a brief pause then Jordan rolled his eyes at me and said cheerfully, 'I'm terribly sorry, I must have the wrong number,' and hung up.

He did that six more times before conceding defeat. 'I guess he's not listed.'

'D'uh!' I said, relieved. 'Man on the run, remember? Shove over, Sherlock.'

I brought up a new window and a different search engine. 'What was her real name? Eve's? Monica *what*?'

Jordan rested an elbow on my knees and it felt so right it

almost took my breath away. While my insides did an unco-ordinated happy dance, Jordan frowned into the screen.

'She didn't introduce herself, if that's what you mean,' he muttered. 'The way I got her name came out of something she showed me. It was dark, really dark, and I saw something, like a, I dunno, path? Beside a river? Running water, anyway, I could hear it, and someone was calling out quietly, like they didn't want anyone else to know— *Mon-ica?Mon-ica?* Like the way you'd call a cat. I could hear footsteps behind her, the sound of his breathing.'

Jordan shivered and I tensed, knowing he was sparing me the full story, all the little Panavision details.

'Try him instead, the O'Loughlin guy,' Jordan murmured, shaking himself. 'I still think he's the key to everything. What's his story? How big a psychopath are we talking here? Just big? Or big *big*?'

Reluctantly, as if typing in the man's name would somehow enable him to see us through my webcam, I did what Jordan asked. I started feeling sick as news stories, weeks old, flashed up: of some outlaw bikie kingpin walking into a strip club at 6.17 one morning and dragging his topless ex-girlfriend, Monica Cybo, straight out of her shift and into a laneway already filling with office workers. There, Keith O'Loughlin shot and killed an innocent man who'd tried to intervene on Monica's behalf, critically wounding a backpacker who also came to her defence. A woman in her car at a set of lights was also hit, but was expected to live.

After that, O'Loughlin and Monica had each vanished into thin air. No one knew what had become of either of them. One reporter speculated that O'Loughlin—head of the Reavers outlaw motorcycle gang—was presently employing a vast, interstate network of bikie brothers-in-arms to stay under the radar and that he was holding Monica somewhere against her will.

But Jordan and I knew something that none of the papers did: Nadja herself had said that Keith O'Loughlin had gone to the Maximus Lounge looking for Monica, *even after what he did*. Somehow, against the odds, she'd gotten away from him that day. But then she'd died and become the thing I'd come to call *Eve*. Had O'Loughlin found Monica after all?

Ice! Vodka shooters! Strippers! Roid Rage!

'She's the one,' I said shakily. 'The one they were all talking about until all that stuff about *me* pushed all that stuff about her right off the telly and the front page. Jesus.'

I studied the grainy black-and-white head shot accompanying the news article. It showed a middle-aged man with a slick pony tail and pronounced widow's peak, taken with a long lens. The quality was hopeless, but it was the only picture on file of the notorious biker. I could feel my teeth chattering and they seemed beyond my control.

'I was right! *He killed her,* Jordan, he must have. That's why no one's seen either of them for weeks. And you just tried to call him direct! What if he finds out?'

I hastily punched the window closed and all the news stories on Keith O'Loughlin vanished, to be replaced by the list of seven *K. O'Loughlin*s we'd found in the residential directory. Revolted, I quickly clicked the *back* button, and one hundred and one *C. Kelly*s from here to the state's borders filled the screen again.

The feeling of wanting to throw up intensified.

'Why did you have to go and die?' I wailed, looking for her in the ancient plaster ceiling rose; in the amber glass teardrop chandelier some colourblind dag had installed in the 1970s; in the dark and dusty corners of my bedroom; but seeing nothing. Oh, I could almost smell her though, almost feel her lurking, waiting to see what we would make of all the crappy, unhelpful little clues she'd let fall our way.

'It's not enough, Eve,' I mumbled, 'give us more.'

I had been about to add: *Damn you,* but bit back the words. That part had already happened.

I was tired. My mouth felt like sawdust and my head seemed filled with molten lead and all I wanted, really, was to crawl back into my bed cave, preferably with Jordan by my side, and never come out.

But *they* have opinions. They possess some animalistic,

residual ability to reason, some kind of low cunning that persists, even after death. I knew that, because of the man in Room 3, with his hatred of the pokies in the Sports Bar that had never existed when he was alive.

If they could reason, they could be goaded.

I sat bolt upright and told Jordan: 'Go get something to eat.'

'Hey?' Jordan replied, surprised, squinting up at me.

'Not much more we can do tonight,' I said, crossing my arms. 'Leave now. Go home.'

Inwardly, I was cringing, remembering the time I'd told Eve to take her problems to someone else and she'd pushed me so hard I'd blacked out. Outwardly, I made my body language so fierce and spiky and unfriendly that any casual observer could see I wanted Jordan gone.

'What?' he said, sounding hurt. 'But we could start calling. It's not even seven yet. There's, what, a hundred Kellys to knock over? And I think we, uh, established that we can handle, um, spending time together. I'm good to go, if you are.'

I noted the faint flush that moved across his cheekbones with interest, but hardening my heart, I snarled, 'We'll do it tomorrow. Or maybe next week. Sure, we'll call every one of those people, but we'll take our time doing it. I mean, no sense hurrying, right? Seeing as she's already old news. What's the goddamned rush? I'm sick of being pushed around by a dead stripper just dumb enough to get herself killed. Now get out of here, J. I like you, but I can't stand being around you right now.'

Jordan stood up, still looking uncertain. He twisted the armbands around one wrist, saying, 'You said so yourself, Soph. It can never wait.'

I could tell from the way he was holding himself that he didn't really want to leave.

But I thought again about the man in Room 3, and what he was doing to our floorboards.

'I've decided it can,' I sniffed dismissively. 'She was a *ho*, Jordan. A lowlife skanky skank. Why even bother, right? We've done enough. This is pointless.'

I felt guilty even before the words left my mouth. 'You know, she probably had it coming. She probably deserved exactly what was done to her.'

Jordan went still like a cornered animal.

I only got the faintest whiff of violets before my entire bedroom vanished around me.

13

It wasn't like the last time: a polite show reel involving strange faces, strange places somehow projected behind my eyes.

No. This time I was *inside* a…memory?

Some tiny part of me registered that I couldn't have moved. Dimly, I still sensed my trainer-shod feet resting on the pitted jarrah floorboards of my bedroom, heard my own laboured breathing in my ears.

But my eyes were telling me that I was standing on a gravel-strewn railway line that cut straight through the heart of a quiet suburban street. The street—hilly, steep and narrow—stretched away from me on either side of the track. It was edged with compact Victorian workers' cottages; the homes built so closely together that they seemed like houses made for little people, mostly of timber, mostly rundown.

I turned to look behind me and saw two small, badly lit train platforms, one on either side of the rails, empty at this hour.

It was dark. So dark: only a few houses along the street had lights on.

Then a single porch light flashed on at the front of the faded blue weatherboard house just down the hill. The place had been built right up against the railway line; the track itself formed one of the property's side boundaries.

The front door swung open and emitted a curvy woman wearing a black tank top and black jeans, flip flops, her long black hair worn unbound and forwards across her shoulders. In the warm porch light I caught a glimpse of a tall, lean shape just inside the open door. The woman leant up on tiptoes and gave the shadowy figure a lingering hug, planting a kiss on the person's pale cheek, before the door was shut behind her.

The woman looked up at the sky before letting herself out the front gate and turning right, away from me standing on the track, almost instantly blending into the night.

I had known who she was instantly.

I tried to call out her name, tried to warn her against leaving the safety of the little blue house, but my throat wouldn't work. I could still feel my bedroom floor through the soles of my shoes, but all my eyes could see were the weeds twining up through the gravel on the railway tracks, all they registered was the flashing of the red signal lights on both sides of the crossing.

I raised my hands to my face and red light pulsed over my skin like a visual representation of my beating heart, and I knew I was inside one of the last moments of Eve's life, unable to prevent the terrible *something* that would happen next.

Until this moment, I'd been deaf to my surroundings. But then a piercing whistle blast caused me to look up, away from my hands, and back at her.

The sound caused Eve to look over her shoulder, too. Then she turned towards the track, towards me. There was a lit match cupped in her hands, a cigarette jammed in one corner of her mouth. For an instant, it seemed as if she looked straight at me. By the light of her flickering match I imagined recognition in her face as we stared at each other across the lowered railway barrier.

Then her features contorted in a fear so terrible I actually recoiled.

She turned and ran down the hill, and I began to move, too. But then a whistle blast sounded so loud and so close in my ears that I only had time to turn and throw up my hands, open my mouth wide to scream, before I was hit by a night express train.

✦

Was I dead?

It seemed forever before I could force my eyelids open.

A dangling frieze of amber glass teardrops hung overhead. They swung gently in the cold drafts that have always plagued the upstairs bedrooms at The Star. Tiny air bubbles were suspended through the glass, and the light the teardrops cast was soft and beautiful. I seemed to be in one piece.

'Am I dead?' I murmured, knowing I couldn't be, because the afterlife would have to have better light fixtures than this.

Jordan expelled a pent-up breath and laughed, a sound warm and lovely.

His face came into view over mine and I realised that my head was resting across his legs.

'This is nice,' I said softly. 'Maybe I *am* dead.'

Jordan's mouth lifted at the corners. 'And now you're haunting *me*? You wish.' His face grew sombre. 'What happened? What did you see?'

The questions sounded normal, coming from him. 'You were standing there, looking frozen,' he said, 'head bent like you were listening. Then you went down like a sack of potatoes.'

I shifted uneasily as I relived the horror. 'I, uh, got hit by an express train.'

'You *what*?'

I told him about the particle of Eve's past that I'd just been immersed in and saw a look of resignation flit across his face. I also told him about the time Eve had caused me to black out when I wouldn't help her.

'It was my fault then, too,' I mumbled. 'I didn't want to help her, she got angry. But tonight, I made her angry on purpose, so that she would show me more. She saw someone that night, when she left that blue house. Someone she knew who frightened her.'

'So when you told me to leave, you weren't really trying to get rid of me then?' Jordan breathed, leaning closer.

But he straightened when I grabbed his arm from below, remembering. 'Jordan, I *heard* the train's whistle. It's, like, when our eyes met inside that memory, Eve switched the sound on for the first time. I've never been able to hear sounds before, you know, when she shows me things. What does it mean that I could...*hear*?'

Jordan frowned. 'I've never heard of that happening; that your "gifts" can get changed or...augmented like that. Daughtry might know why that is. I'll have to ask him.'

I swallowed, remembering the front grille of the

speeding, phantom express train. 'Do you think whoever was chasing her…died?'

Jordan helped me sit up. 'That part's easy enough to check. Let's see if there's any word of a fatality at a suburban rail crossing, say, in the last month.'

He pushed me off his legs, suddenly eager to know, because it gave us a shortcut into that list of Kellys my computer had spat out before. Maybe.

While Jordan crossed to my computer, I hugged my knees to my chest, my bum still on the floorboards, head still pounding with the frantic ghost echoes of that railway signal.

'If we find the right crossing, we'll find Carter Kelly and the blue house,' he said, sinking down in front of the screen and starting to type.

But as he tried a handful of different search angles, I saw his shoulders slump.

'Nothing involving a pedestrian and a railway crossing in the last few weeks,' he muttered, shoving his fringe out of his eyes. 'There were two involving cars, but they occurred in broad daylight. Whoever was chasing her couldn't have died.'

'How about going back and looking for suburban railway lines that cut through residential areas?'

'Good idea,' Jordan replied, fingers already moving on the keys.

My bedroom door opened abruptly and I turned. Gran—with a plate piled high with food—looked down at me on the floor, then across the room at Jordan, who'd swung around in my desk chair, wide-eyed at the sudden interruption.

'You really *are* doing research,' she murmured in disbelief. 'Thought I'd have to lever you two apart with a crowbar. Brought sandwiches. Figured you'd be hungry.'

She set the plate down beside Jordan's right arm then came back and stood over me, saying softly, 'You look like hell, pet. Can't this wait till you're feeling better?'

I shook my head, too tired to pick myself up off the floor as Jordan walked over and handed me a sandwich with Cook's pungent curried-egg salad mashed in between the two triangles of white bread. I wrinkled my nose at it before taking a bite, feeling uncomfortable as Gran and Jordan continued to stare down at me like I was something squashed onto the floor.

I almost choked when Jordan said, 'She needs looking after, Mrs Teague.'

'That she does,' Gran agreed, regarding Jordan gravely over her reading glasses. 'About bloody time one of you blokes took notice.'

She took a deep breath, then said with a forced air of casualness, 'It's getting real late, Jordan, so you've got two choices. Head on home and come back first thing or, when you've finished up on the computer, take your pick of the upstairs bedrooms'—Jordan's eyes widened in surprise as Gran added smoothly—'save for those rooms already occupied, of course.'

'Of course, Mrs Teague,' Jordan said. 'Thank you, that's, uh, very kind of you. I'll just call Mum and let her know what I'm doing. Soph and I are working on something together that can't wait. It's important.'

'It's always important,' Gran snorted, 'until the next bloody thing comes along. Just remember that.'

She helped me up off the floor and I sank down on the edge of my bed gratefully, watching as Jordan took out his mobile phone and laid it on the edge of my desk.

Gran stood looking at me for a moment more. 'Just be careful,' she said. 'I don't know what you're up to and I don't *want* to know, but don't go putting yourself in harm's way, love. Your karma's good enough and we don't need any more free publicity...'

She bustled out the door, calling back over her shoulder, 'I'll put towels in the aqua bathroom, Soph, show him where it is, and get some sleep, for God's sake. You're not well.'

In the background, Jordan finished his call to his mum and laid his phone back on my desk.

'She's cool, your Gran,' he said, sliding back into my desk chair.

All I could think was: *He's staying the night. Just wait until that gets out*.

Claudia P. was going to pummel me extra, for sure.

Because if you'd told me that the untouchable Jordan Haig and I would go from zero to sleepovers in the space of a single day, I would've said you'd obviously checked your brain at the door and someone had trod on it in the bargain. But here we were.

'What did you find on those train stations?' I countered.

Jordan turned back to the screen. 'Describe the house again,' he said. 'We need to narrow down the number of stations that cut through residential streets then match them against the Kellys that are publicly listed.'

It sounded like a big job, and I told him so with my eyebrows, but Jordan shrugged. 'We have to start somewhere, right?'

I told him again that the house had looked the same general vintage as our pub. 'Victorian, you know, 19th century. But low ceilings, and timber, because it was built as a residence, not a public house. Everything in the street packed in tight, all built shoulder-to-shoulder. So, yeah, working class. Old. It was blue, had a hip-high picket fence with a gate in the middle, no off-street parking.'

While I talked, Jordan printed out the list of C. Kellys we'd found and handed it to me together with a red pen he'd found by rootling around on top of my messy desk.

'What you're describing is inner city,' he mused. 'Could be any direction though, but I'd discount anything that isn't close to a river of some kind. I'm thinking the Maribyrnong River, or the Yarra.'

'You're sure?' I said uncertainly. 'Eve never showed me a river.'

Jordan's expression went bleak. 'I'm sure. You know how she gave you a taster of what her last moments were like? I've had those, too, but different ones. A river figures in there somewhere, trust me. Given the type of house we're looking for, cross out all the names and addresses that are outside the inner-Metropolitan area, then give us back that list, okay?'

Jordan typed away on my laptop while I did what he asked.

'Where's Bittern?' I queried.

He shook his head. 'On the Mornington Peninsula, I think. Holiday houses for rich people. Lose that one.'

When I was done, I had a list of nine.

'Give it here,' Jordan said, as he studied the high-lighted possibilities.

He brought up all the *C. Kelly*s again on the screen and started clicking on the first one.

I went and stood over his shoulder. 'There's a *map* option,' I pointed out. 'I didn't know you could do that, pull a person's location up on a map. That's kind of…freaky.'

'And intrusive,' Jordan muttered. 'But useful.'

One-by-one, flicking between directory view and street view, we started ruling people out. Dejection started creeping back into our voices as we talked over each other.

'No train line.'

'No bodies of water.'

'Houses are too new.'

'Blocks are too big.'

'Lots of light industrial.'

'Borderline too far out, don't you think?'

The seventh set of details was for a place in Northcote, not far from where we were now.

When the street map came up, Jordan moodily flicked straight to the satellite imaging for the area. 'Look at this,' he snarled. 'Street after friggin' street of same-same. Do you want *ant* view? Or *God* view?'

I punched him in the shoulder. 'Zoom out,' I insisted. 'More. *More.*'

'God view it is, then.'

I stared at the patterns of light and dark on the screen, all the tiny, photo-realistic little houses that from this magnification looked like pieces from a board game. Something about the satellite imagery for the Northcote *C. Kelly* was bothering me, though. Cutting down through the left edge of the map and snaking across the bottom was a lush, dark-green line. The curvy line was punctuated by the green of public parks and reserves. I was looking at ovals, playgrounds, walks. Kilometres of them.

So much…green.

Including the dark green of *trees*, I realised.

'Trees that need water,' I muttered aloud.

'What?' Jordan hadn't seen it. Maybe I was wrong.

'Go back to the directory view,' I begged. 'You know, the pastel, cartoony one.'

'Why?' Jordan exclaimed. 'I still don't know what I'm looking at.'

I shoved him aside and bent over the keyboard, clicking back into the stylised road map for the area and jabbing at the screen with one finger.

The screen was suddenly colour-coded and artificial-looking again, *cartoony*, just like I'd said. And covered in tiny names that explained everything. Every single thing we were looking at was *labelled*. Street names, parks, walks, *everything*.

'You're supposed to be *gifted*,' I said dryly, tapping the bottom of the screen. What had been dark green in the photographic view had morphed into a dull, pale-green sward, cut through by a thin ribbon of *blue*.

'Water,' Jordan whispered, astonished.

'Merri Creek,' I muttered. 'And a train line runs right through the area.'

I pointed out Rushall Station. And the string of little stations that ran north above it.

'There are more,' I said, excitedly pointing to the east of the image. 'A different train line, that intersects with the other one, once you hit Clifton Hill. They all look like small, unmanned stations. Just like the one I saw. Completely deserted in the dark. You could imagine trains going straight through them in the night—express, no stops.'

Jordan fumbled for the list of *Kelly*s again and peered intently at the address details for lucky contestant number seven.

'There should be a little marker,' I reminded him breathlessly, 'pinpointing the guy's exact location.'

I broke out in goose bumps when Jordan found it. A narrow grey train track cut straight through the heart of that person's street and the marker stood right alongside the point of intersection. The Northcote *C. Kelly* lived in a house next to a railway line.

I hugged myself, feeling chilled. 'This is the one,' I muttered. 'Bring up the house. I want to see it.'

Back in satellite view, we studied the magnified image of a faded blue, single-storey, Victorian timber place with a picket fence in a matching blue and a pocket-sized front garden that faced onto a narrow street packed with houses of a similar condition and calibre. I grabbed control of the mouse off Jordan and angled up and down the street, clicking to bring myself closer to the railway crossing that was just uphill from the front of the property.

As I looked up and down the tracks, mentally overlaying the things I'd seen with the static daylight images on the screen, my body went colder. I zoomed back out and stared at the surrounding area.

'Any of the streets to the east of that one could take you down to Merri Creek. If it was dark, and you were scared and running, it would be easy to lose your way and forget where the main drags are and get lost in all the bush around there...'

I circled an area at the bottom of the screen with a shaky finger.

Jordan seemed to come to some sort of decision and drew my hands down so that his face was inches from mine. 'No heroics. It's almost midnight. We'll tackle it in daylight, okay? And I'll tell plenty of people where we're going in case Carter Kelly turns out to be another one of Eve's psycho exes.'

He rested his forehead against mine and I closed my eyes.

'You're tired and I'm tired,' he murmured, 'and we're not going to start this now when she's here, muddying everything, watching over us. But we will start it. We have already. Something from nothing. A fricken miracle.'

He gave me a feather-light kiss before pushing himself up out of my chair and leaving my room so quickly and quietly that all I could discern, through my still closed eyelids, was the sound of the door snicking shut behind him.

14

The sound was repetitive, insistent. Electronic? But, still, I refused to let go of sleep.

I'd been dreaming of something that had turned into the sound of this…thing.

It fell silent, and I felt myself relax back down, digging for the remnants of the dream—Dad and me, as a kid. At a lavender farm high on a hill that had every flower you could imagine growing there, with a glimpse of the ocean shining at its boundaries. I'd forgotten that place. He'd been leading me by the hand, wanting to show me something and I'd wanted to see, to see—

But then, a bare second later, the buzzing started again.

Cracking my eyelids open at last, I fell out of bed onto

my knees and lunged upwards, feeling for the insistent, buzzing shape on my desk.

The fluorescent face of my alarm clock said it was 2.33am. I found myself holding Jordan's trembling mobile in my hand because he'd left it in here, along with his beat-up leather jacket, still slung over the back of my chair.

I hadn't dreamt him up then. He really was right down the hall.

I picked up the call, muttered: 'Hello?'

'Sophie?' The voice on the end of the line was warm. Seductive. Male. Devastating, with a hint of something. French, maybe? I'm no good with accents.

I cleared my throat. 'Uh, this is Jordan's phone.' It struck me a second later, still foggy from sleep. 'How'd you know my name?'

The stranger laughed, and it sent shivers straight down my spine. 'Charmian—Jordan's mother—told me you'd be together. You sound intriguing, Sophie.'

As usual my brain ran ahead of my mouth. 'I don't feel intriguing. Do you know what time it is? Want me to get him? He's asleep.'

The man on the other end chuckled, and I coloured instantly, even though he couldn't see me.

'Um, not in here,' I gabbled. 'I meant, ah, Jordan's sleeping, but in another room altogether. Down the hall. I can get him. If you want.'

I sounded like a five-year-old with poor linguistic abilities.

'Please, Sophie,' the man drawled, 'if you would. I need to talk to him. I have a message. I can't say that I understand it, but it's very urgent.'

'Uh, okay.'

I pushed my door open and peered down the hall, feeling the hairs on my body rising at the sight of Room 3 in the distance, the winking jukebox beyond it.

A man had died in that room and was still, by all accounts, residing there. My God, what had my life come to?

Thankfully, Jordan had chosen a room down the other way, between my room and Gran's, and I didn't have to walk past the *Orange Room* in the dark.

I still had Jordan's phone pressed to my ear and was feeling around for my oversized bunny slippers with my toes, when the stranger said again, 'Sophie?'

I jumped and almost dropped the phone. There was warmth in his voice still, but also a steely edge in his next words.

'Get him, please? *Hurry.*'

Flustered, I murmured, 'Hold on a minute, okay?' and shuffled out my door.

As I made my way down the cold hallway, I heard the fat, muted *blat blat* of a Harley moving down the street.

Dad had had one to the end, and I recognised the peculiar timbre of its engine, that underlying threat of power. It must have done a U-turn, because I heard it circling outside then go back the way it had come, before the sound faded out of hearing.

I reached Jordan's door and tapped tentatively. Even though Gran generally slept like a woman in a coma, all that separated his room from hers was a tiled, 1970s-era bathroom redolent of the electric blue of peacock feathers. If I ever did work up enough nerve to put the moves on Jordan Haig, it wasn't going to happen within spitting distance of Gran, or The Star. Nothing could be less romantic than this place. It was home, but it was falling apart. Dad just saw it through rose-coloured glasses, and when he was alive, we had too.

Nothing stirred behind the door so, still knocking, I pushed it open slowly, hissing in the direction of the lump on the bed, 'Jordan? *Jordan?* Phone call. Urgent.'

There was a creak of bedsprings at last, and Jordan trailed out of the darkness into the doorway. He was yawning and wearing a white V-necked T-shirt and black boxers and nothing else, his dark hair standing on end like ruffled quills.

I held his phone out to him as if he were mildly contagious, and shuffled back out of reach, just in case Gran had her beady eye planted in the crack of her doorway.

'Phone,' I repeated nervously, telling myself to *look away*, *look away* from the long, bare, muscular expanse of his legs. It wasn't helping that I was standing here in a pair of blue flannel pyjamas with pink and purple smiling cats printed on them, a couple of large, stuffed rabbits on my feet, my hair a ginger explosion.

Jordan glanced at the phone in his hand blearily then held it up to his ear.

'Hello?' His voice was sleep-roughened and uncertain.

Quite clearly, I heard the man on the line say, 'Jordan?'

Jordan's dark eyebrows shot up and he looked at me in concern, every trace of sleepiness gone. 'Daughtry? What are you doing back? And why are you calling *now*?'

I saw Jordan's gaze go to the street-facing windows behind my back, then sharpen. 'Is it Mum? Is she in trouble? Is that why you're calling?'

Daughtry's answering laugh was faintly quizzical. 'No, no, nothing like that, my friend, she's very well. We just spoke. No, I called for you. There is a message; it is urgent, I think. *You must stay down.* Does that make sense? That you must get down, get out of the way?'

There was a sudden mechanical roar; like a jumbo jet was taking off out the front of The Star. A sustained rumbling you could almost feel going up through the walls and floorboards.

Jordan moved towards me, instinctively, still holding

the phone to his ear. But I stood stock still, recognising the sound because I'd only just heard it. It was the sound of a Harley; only magnified. There were lots of them, I realised, moving down Sancerre Street in formation, going fast, engines revving.

Jordan's eyes flew to mine and he dropped the phone, pulling me to him so fiercely that he fell over backwards onto the floor, with me sprawled across his body.

I felt the breath leave him in a *whoosh* and heard Daughtry's voice, small and tinny, shouting: 'Jordan? *Jordan*!' a split second before shots rang out.

All the windows along the face of our hotel shattered inwards, filling the air where I'd just been standing with the smell of gunpowder and rain, and the sound of Gran screaming my name.

✦

The police interviews—conducted in the Public Bar with appropriate refreshments—took hours.

'Daughtry can be our backup when we go see Carter Kelly,' Jordan had insisted as the police had finished up their search of Sancerre Street and the surrounding neighbourhood and indicated that they wished to speak with me.

'You think that's wise?' I hissed out the side of my

mouth, as a large man in dark blue crooked an index finger at me. 'He's just one guy.'

'Who can handle himself and every man, woman or unquiet spirit you could hope to come across,' Jordan shot back. 'You have to see Daughtry to understand what I'm talking about. He knows *stuff*, I'm telling you. He has skills. That sharpened stick he wears in his hair? He knows how to *use* it on people. I've seen him. A couple of drunks took Daughtry and me on one night in the street and he, I dunno, disabled them with it. Smashed the end of it into one man's collarbone, hit some pressure points in the other dude's head and neck and he went down and stayed down. I didn't even have time to react and we were already walking away.'

I shook my head in disbelief.

'Eve wants it this way,' Jordan insisted. '*Us* handling it. She came to you. She didn't go to them.' He nodded at the waiting police officers who were finishing up with Gran and her take on events.

'I'm betting that when she was alive,' Jordan added, 'Eve wouldn't have gone near the police if she could help it. We "gathered" the shirt, just as she wanted, and now we hand it over to Carter Kelly. That's all the orders we have. If there's anything else, Daughtry's back in town. *He* can handle Eve, and the cops can do the rest, and we bow out, having done all we humanly can.'

'And if the drop-off goes bad?' I'd said sourly, 'we'll either be dead or need witness protection from the Reavers and their associates. The Reavers drink at the Maximus Lounge, Roman said as much. Which means that Roman must have told O'Loughlin we paid a visit, and this is the way they return a favour.'

'At least we'll be together,' Jordan had murmured with a crooked smile as I took a seat beside Gran. 'Look at the positives.'

Jordan adjusted the sleeves on his leather jacket carefully, so that his arms were covered up past his wrists, before taking the seat beside mine on the other side. 'Boyfriend,' he responded so confidently to the officers' looks of enquiry that the word did terrible things to my heart.

'We'll get to you later, chief,' said the officer who'd introduced himself to me earlier as Senior Constable Ben Ferguson. He was tall, square-shouldered and square-jawed, clean-shaven with cropped curly brown hair and blue eyes. If he wasn't a policeman, and kind of old, I would have described him as fairly hot. The other one was a ranga like me, lean-built, with bad acne scars all over his narrow face and watchful brown eyes. He looked like a fifteen-year-old who'd stolen someone's uniform as a joke.

The two men made me go back through the Crime Stoppers stuff, everything: what I was doing out at all those places, how I could even have known about them. They even called the cops I'd spoken with each of the other times, trying to link it all together with what had gone down overnight at The Star.

Of course, any idiot could tell you none of it was remotely believable; even though it was all true.

And the whole time, Jordan held my hand, tight, and I never breathed a word about what *he* could do. Or about Eve, who *was* the link.

I just kept insisting it was *visions*. I'd just suddenly started having visions. I even told them the date and the time when it all began, what song I'd been listening to. I even tumbled to the ghostly visitation when I was five: the man in the plaid shirt, jeans and boots, gleaming in the darkness. I'd felt Jordan's shock in the sudden crushing pressure he'd applied to my hand. It was the first time I'd told the story to anyone.

'You've been holding out on me,' he said in a low, strained voice.

'Nothing normal about me,' I'd murmured in agreement as the police concluded that the common link was *me*—not Eve, no mention made of dead strippers—the way I meant them to.

Jordan and I hadn't had much time to talk since we'd hit the decks and gotten showered in a tonne of glass. But we had no proof Keith O'Loughlin and the Reavers had been behind tonight's drive by aeration of The Star's 142-year-old façade. We'd hastily agreed that pointing fingers in his direction would only get us definitively killed, as opposed to nearly. Because tonight had been a warning: to stop digging around in the business of a deranged man, and walk away.

After I was done talking, Ferguson leaned back in his chair, folding his arms across his big, broad chest, and told Gran without a hint of irony: 'You've got a special girl, here. And excepting the childhood…incident, she's had no history of these, eh, visions until about a month ago, you say?'

Gran nodded, confounded.

'I had no idea,' she said, flustered, 'truly. She never said. But it explains a lot.'

She turned and looked at me, her heart in her eyes, sitting there so tense it looked like she might snap in half.

The two police officers gazed around the Public Bar. 'Bit of a pile to run, I imagine,' said Constable Watts, the ranga, staring up at the ceiling. 'But it's got a solid rep, this place. A few drunk and disorderlies from time to time. But nothing like this has ever happened before…?'

Gran shook her head, face crumpling. 'It was my late husband's dream,' she said. 'And we honour dreams in this family, even if it means getting shot up. Keeping this place going…he wouldn't have wanted to be remembered any other way. It's how I keep him close.'

Jordan squeezed my hand and I squeezed Gran's and she nodded, still staring at her knees sightlessly. She'd put her dingy grey and pink tracksuit on over her short yellow nightie, and her blonde, spiky hair looked like a rat's nest. But her posture was stiff and straight, like a queen's.

Both officers cleared their throats, turning back to me.

Constable Watts narrowed his dark eyes shrewdly. 'Working on anything now? Anything, say, that would get up the noses of an outlaw bikie gang?'

I felt sick as Gran clutched my fingers tight enough to cut off my circulation. 'Soph?' she breathed.

I turned and looked at her—could see her thinking about Dad and his past connections, *the troubles*, as she called the period preceding Joss' hasty return to the fold with a ready-made family.

But after a moment she let go of my hand and sat on, saying nothing. All I knew, from what I'd ever managed to get out of Mum, was that no man ever 'left' the Reavers. *It's the brotherhood you take to your grave*, she had laughed once, almost giddy with relief. *But your dad managed to get out. And it was bad, the getting out, but he did it and here we are!*

But Gran never talked about what the leaving had actually taken—and she didn't now. It was almost two decades ago; Dad as a bikie henchman fringe dweller was so ancient history, I could see her thinking that it made no sense bringing it up now. And, feeling like a coward, I stayed silent, too.

The constable prompted me again as the silence lengthened. 'Anything new "coming through" right now?'

'Nope, nothing new coming through right now,' I parroted as Jordan gave my hand a tiny squeeze.

Which was true. Nothing new.

'Then what were you two doing upstairs on the computer?' Gran interrupted. 'You said it was important, what you were working on. It's no time for secrets, Soph. Tell them if it's put you in danger.'

Constable Watts turned to Jordan saying pleasantly, 'Anything we should know about?'

I looked at Jordan, not trusting myself to speak.

'We just had a T-shirt and a card to deliver, to a friend,' Jordan said evenly. 'Soph and me spent last night looking up his place and arranging how to get there. It's in Northcote. It's urgent, it had to go today or we'd be late with it, but...'

Jordan lifted his chin in the direction of the street-facing windows. There was a scrum of reporters barricaded outside, across the street, all trying to get pictures with their long-lens cameras of us sitting in here having tea and ribbon sandwiches with the police. Anytime anyone came in or out of the building they'd stir like a school of piranha, all pointing in the same direction, mouths open, teeth flashing, ready to strip people of information.

Ferguson laughed scornfully. 'It's seeing members of Task Force Brigand poking around that's got them all excited.'

He swung his bright-blue gaze back to me. 'That, and the fact you seem to have a habit of making good Christian folk really nervous, young Sophie Teague. You're great TV. People are beginning to say you're in league with the Devil. Want a word with him, too, if you can manage that. Have a few questions.'

Ferguson snorted at his own joke while I flushed miserably.

'I didn't ask for this, and that's the truth. I wish it would go away.'

'We—ell,' Ferguson drew out the word as he flipped shut his police-issue notebook, 'if any of your "visions" end up telling you why a bunch of lawless bikies took it upon themselves to shoot up your granny's establishment just before three in the morning, you give us a call, hmmm? But in the meantime…'

I looked up and saw him exchange a fleeting glance with Constable Watts. 'How about we get you to your friend's place to deliver that T-shirt in time for his birthday, hey?'

Jordan's head came up. 'Seriously? That would be awesome.'

I looked at Jordan uncertainly. 'I'm not sure Carter would want us turning up with…'

'Your friend Carter have a last name?' Constable Watts interjected, jamming his police hat back on and rising.

'It's *Kelly*,' Jordan called back over his shoulder, already heading upstairs. 'Wait a minute while I get it.'

As if he'd lost interest in the whole catastrophe, Constable Watts wandered away and out through the front door. Ferguson finished his cup of tea and engulfed Gran's hand in his. 'If anything comes to mind, Mrs Teague,' he said, 'you've got our numbers.'

She nodded, indicating me with a tilt of her head. 'And thank you, for getting her to her friend's place. I wasn't going to let her out of my sight today.'

'All part of the service, ma'am,' Ferguson smiled before telling me he'd arrange to have a car round the back for us as soon as the Task Force finished up.

When the officers were out of earshot, Gran said in a low voice, 'Is that really what you're doing? Delivering a present? If it were up to me, I'd chain you to the end of your bed and never let you out again if it would keep you safe. *Outlaw bikies*, Sophie, *Christ*. I thought I'd seen the back of them for good. What have you done, my girl, what have you *done*?'

Unable to frame an answer that would alleviate her worry, I was glad when Jordan chose that precise moment to lope back into view holding the wrinkled plastic bag.

'I'll show you, Gran,' I said, relieved. 'Look. It's just a T-shirt. Honest.'

A little of Gran's tension eased when she caught sight of the shirt and blue envelope. Jordan had taken the time to seal the card inside it so that the *Thank you!* message Eve had once written was no longer visible to contradict us.

'Bit gay-designer-pirate, isn't it?' Gran sniffed, looking the shirt over, before heading into the office to call the glass repairmen.

✦

We didn't leave until after 2pm. Gran even had chicken parmas sent out to all the forensic guys combing the footpaths and drains outside, because she didn't have to look after the usual ferals.

'All set, you two?' Senior Constable Ferguson said gruffly as the police car clattered out through Sancerre Lane and past the waiting sea of reporters before any of them could get wind of us crouching in the back seat footwells.

'At Rae Street,' he added, over his shoulder, sternly, 'it's seat belts, no arguments.'

We did as we were told over the intermittent buzz of radio chatter.

Both men had given the card and tee only a cursory glance at The Star, but I knew from the way Ferguson was driving that they'd run Carter Kelly's official stats. They'd never even asked us what his address was, but here we were on St Georges Road crossing Holden Street in the direction of Northcote.

I caught a glimpse of rushing water out my window and shoved an elbow into Jordan's ribs. He was playing with his phone, and I knew he was texting Daughtry that we were almost there. I was curious to see this paragon with the sexy voice and ability to banish the dead.

I went cold as the car bumped across the railway line and I caught sight of the concrete station platforms going past. They hugged the track to my right, looking grey-on-grey in the wintry light. A girl with bobbed, purple hair in a vintage dress, striped stockings and an oversized green mohair cardigan, turned her head sharply and stared at us going by in the police car, before refocusing her gaze on the empty platform opposite.

We pulled up across the road from the single-fronted, faded blue timber house on Branxholme Street. I pretended not to notice Senior Constable Ferguson's steady gaze in the driver's mirror as he said dryly, 'Best home before dark, children.'

Jordan had to open my door and help me out because my legs weren't really working. It was the usual shock, you see, of having something move out of the realm of the perceived, into the real.

This was the place.

Somehow, I'd done it again. I was outside the house Eve had shown me. I was actually here.

15

It looked and smelt like rain was coming as we pushed our way through the front gate and walked the short path to the door, stepping up under the verandah. Jordan had the rolled up plastic bag in one hand.

Behind us, I heard the police car's engine idling while we rang the bell. I glanced over my shoulder as Ferguson did a noisy three-point turn and roared back the way we'd come, one large hand briefly raised in our direction.

The door was the same chipped and faded blue as the rest of the house. No one came to answer it, and after a polite pause, Jordan leant on the buzzer again, only longer this time. I thought maybe I saw the edge of a curtain twitch in the front window to the right of the door, but I couldn't be sure. Jordan's mobile chose that moment to let off a melodic three-note pinging that indicated a message.

He stared down at the screen with a heavy frown. 'Daughtry wants me to meet him at the station. That's weird: I thought I made it pretty clear about when and where to get off.' Jordan glanced up the hill towards the cheerless platforms we'd only just driven past. 'Says he's only a few stops away.'

He shoved his phone back inside his jacket.

'Come on,' he sighed. 'Daughtry's not from here. I have to go get him. It's like Mum says: when you expect him he doesn't show, and when you don't, he just materialises out of nowhere.'

There was that almost twitch of a curtain again in the front window, like someone was standing beyond the glass to the right, just listening, hoping we'd go away. The words tumbled out before I'd really thought them through.

'You go,' I was astonished to hear myself say. 'I'll just wait here and keep trying, yeah?'

Jordan looked sceptical. 'No one's here,' he said. 'We'll get Daughtry first then work out what to do about this.' He raised the scrunched up plastic bag in his hand and his mouth twisted wryly. 'Eve didn't give us instructions in the event of no one being home.'

'Leave it with me,' I insisted as a light, furry rain began to fall beyond the decorative edge of the verandah. 'It'll be drier, at least. And I'm just getting over a cold, remember?'

I held out my hand, hoping my smile looked natural, and Jordan handed me the bag.

'No sense both of us getting wet,' he agreed.

He reached out and cupped my cheek, grinning as I flushed.

'I should be able to keep an eye on you from the platform anyway, seeing as it's so close. If anyone comes to the door, just keep them talking until I get back with Daughtry, okay? He can translate stuff from dead languages into workable English, but he can't use public transport. It's unreal.'

Without warning, Jordan leant in and stole a kiss before he turned and clattered back down the steps and up the path.

Face hot as the sun, I held the bag to my knotted-up stomach as Jordan gave me a laconic salute and a slow-burning smile that promised *more later*, before turning in the direction of the railway crossing.

As he moved out of view down a narrow, scrub-lined pedestrian walkway that lay between the edge of Carter Kelly's property and the gravel-strewn track, I turned back and studied the front door with its blank, frosted window set at head height.

Taking a couple of deep, steadying breaths, I pressed

the doorbell five times in succession to indicate I was serious. 'I know you're home,' I called out. 'Open up, please.'

This time, I didn't imagine the hand that drew the front curtain to one side before letting it fall. A dark outline moved into the edges of the frosted glass, and I regarded it the same way I knew whoever was in there was looking at mine.

'No, thanks,' a guy called out finally. 'Not buying.' He sounded young, with a high, clear voice.

'Not selling!' I shouted back, but the shape was already receding backwards in the glass.

Desperate not to lose sight of the shadow beyond the door, I yelled out, 'Carter? *Carter?* Monica sent me. She has something for you.'

I saw the dark shape freeze.

I held the green plastic bag up high in front of my face so that it loomed in the rippled glass.

'How do you know my name? Who sent you?'

'Monica did. Nothing threatening. She even wrote you a card. It's right here. Read it.'

I almost didn't catch his next words. 'That's impossible.' His tone was fearful. 'Monica's *dead*.'

He sounded so certain that I found myself shouting, 'You kill her, Carter? Is that how you know for sure she's dead?'

I leapt back in shock as the door pulled open, the security chain protesting loudly, the wood of the door almost splintering under the force. The guy rasped through the crack, 'Leave me alone or I'll call the police! I didn't kill anyone. You have no proof she was even here. *Go away.*'

All I could see was part of the man's face and one large, frightened blue eye inexplicably outlined in black, liquid eyeliner and three shades of eye shadow, long dark lashes thickly coated with mascara, all expertly applied.

'I came here in a police car, Carter,' I replied calmly. 'Feel free to call them. You'll have some explaining to do.'

The eye shrank back. 'What do they know?' he breathed through the gap separating us.

'All I told them was that you were my friend, and that I was bringing you a birthday present. That's all. I had to be inventive. They seemed to believe me because they've gone.' I saw Carter swallow and shocked myself by adding, 'Can I come in?'

It was clear that Carter was terrified. And part of me— the not kicking myself part—knew it was the right thing to do. I just had to give him one lousy bag. He didn't need three strangers in his house when one would do well enough to hand over Eve's parting gift. It was such a simple thing, and it was still daylight outside and I had a working phone. Plus, Jordan was only an ear-piercing scream away. What could happen?

The young man behind the door didn't move. I could feel the seconds lengthening as he regarded me from head to toe with that single, frightened eye. I could see him taking in my wild, curling mass of ginger hair pulled back into the usual low, loose ponytail; my cold-reddened nose and universal high school dork's ensemble of jeans, runners, pink velour hoodie and sleeveless black puffer. I knew I looked about as threatening as a stick insect in a wig.

Carter caught me by surprise when he blinked, suddenly drawing back into the shadows. In desperation, I held out the plastic bag, trying to shove it through the gap. Maybe just dropping it over Carter's damned threshold would be enough to satisfy Eve, and maybe then the spell she had over me, over Jordan, would be broken and normal transmission would resume.

'At least take this!' I begged. 'It's for you. I don't know why, but she really wants you—*needs* you—to have it. All of it has been leading up to *you*, and I have so many questions, but mostly what I want to know is: *Why?* Why didn't you report her missing when you were, like, one of the last people to see her alive?'

I thought about that memory of hers that I'd found myself standing in. That look on her face. She'd known. She'd known right then and there that she was doomed.

'Monica left your house one night and she never came

back, did she? Who got her?'

'Who *are* you?' he whispered. 'How do you know all these things? How did you find me?'

'Let me come in,' I replied quietly, 'and I'll tell you.'

He regarded me warily for a moment longer. Then I heard the sound of the chain being pushed down a runnel. The door swung open wider to reveal a tall, thin young man with a riot of curly brown hair chopped off at the shoulders. He had a pronounced Adam's apple, the beginnings of a five o'clock shadow and was wearing ripped jeans, a faded grey T-shirt with a complicated sword-and-rose design on it, and bare feet. Carter had the narrowest shoulders I'd ever seen on a man, and the made-up, haunted eyes of a showgirl. I knew I was staring. A guy in full eye makeup with a lush man-fro wouldn't survive to recess at Ivy Street High.

I decided that Carter's face was beautiful: neither fully male nor female, but a strange hybrid of strength and softness.

But then his eyes reddened, and tears spilled down his cheeks, leaving makeup running in long streaks down the perfect oval of his face.

'I never said anything,' he sniffed, 'because I was afraid. People might think I'd done it. Or they'd come after *me*. And Mon always liked men who were dangerous. *Like fire*, she said so herself.' Carter's voice was beseeching. 'You have to understand—she disappeared into thin air and I had no one to tell—by the time I realised she wasn't coming back, it was already too late. I didn't want her here in the first place, but she had nowhere else to go…and I owed her. She used to say that showgirl freaks like us need to stick together.'

Carter began to cry in earnest then, cradling the battered plastic bag against him, really going for it. And I had to look away, because the sound of a man sobbing has to be one of the worst sounds in the world. They don't do it enough so when they do, it sounds rusty and wrong.

'We'd been arguing a lot, she wasn't easy to live with; Mon wasn't easy, period,' Carter blubbered. 'When she didn't come back, the first couple of nights, I tried to convince myself that she'd crashed at someone else's place. *But she left her ring behind*,' he wailed suddenly. 'It creeped me out that thing: I told her it looked like a dead woman's face. But she loved it because her mother had it made for her, back when they were still talking.'

I went cold inside as he added, 'She hardly ever took it off. She never went anywhere without it. But that night, she left it on her bedside table because she hadn't meant to be gone for long. Said she needed to do something. I told her to be careful, but she'd done it before: walked out on her own, at night. How was I supposed to know?'

'Where's the ring now?' I asked feverishly, remembering

the feel of the thing in my hand, so cold and real; the old woman with the long streaks of pure silver in her hair, the grief-ravaged face, shaking her old cross at me.

Carter hugged the bag to himself, sobbing. 'I don't know! It just lay on the table for weeks, I couldn't touch it, could barely look at it. Then, one morning, it was gone. I looked everywhere for it.'

He suddenly reached out and pulled me across the threshold. Reflex made me rear back in his grasp and I caught the heavy scent of rose oil and hair wax mingling with the tang of musky, male sweat. As we struggled, I got a confused impression of a sewing machine in the room to my right, yellow feathers trailing out of a brown cardboard box, and a threadbare Persian runner stretching away into the inner gloom of the house.

'I didn't kill her,' he insisted, still shaking me. 'You have to believe me.'

'Let go of me, Carter,' I warned, flailing around inside my puffer vest for my phone. 'I've got a friend about twenty metres away, watching us. Catch the news, lately? You do anything to me, you'll be famous. Every one of Monica's mad, bad, dangerous friends will know who you are, and where you live. The police will find out you were probably the last person who ever saw her alive, and that you never called them, you coward. Now *get off me*.'

Abruptly, Carter released me and staggered back,

clutching the damned bag like it was plugging a bleeding hole in his abdomen.

'It's proof,' he wept. '*You're* proof.'

'What are you talking about?'

'Last night,' he gabbled, looking wildly up at the ceiling, 'last night…'

I glanced back towards the open front door hoping for some sign, any sign of Jordan and the big blond Viking he'd described, Daughtry. A Viking would be useful right now. 'Go on,' I said more gently.

Carter took a deep, shuddering breath before saying, 'I *asked* her to show me what she wanted because I didn't understand. Things had been happening, small things I could've imagined, I couldn't be sure…and then she sent…*you.*'

He stared at me, appalled, spent tears meshing his impossible eyelashes together in clumps. 'Don't you understand?' he added, as dawning comprehension rearranged the features of my face.

Carter held up the plastic bag I'd come to loathe, and shook it at me.

'I wanted proof she was dead. And she sent you.'

✦

After Carter closed the door, we sat in the front room with

the sewing machine and feathers in it. As I looked around the room, chock full of life-size dressmaking mannequins in various stages of glittering undress and the discarded man-sized stilettos to match, the link between Eve and Carter went crystal clear. What had he called them both? *Showgirls.*

I watched Carter open the bag like it was an unexploded grenade and tear open the card with shaking fingers. His face crumpled again into tears as he read and re-read the brief message inside.

'How?' he whispered, wiping at his face.

I told him everything that had happened to me up until I came to be sitting here in his front room.

'She suddenly showed up,' I snorted softly, 'she bloody chopped up the pieces of my boring, tiny life and threw them in the air for her own enjoyment.'

This made Carter smile for the first time.

'Monica was only ever about number one,' he said quietly. 'Never did a good deed in her life that didn't do a good deed back. *Hated* cats, hated kids. Detested old people, never apologised. But you're saying she's had you crossing town tying up loose ends, doing good deeds. Visiting her *mother*. It's unbelievable.'

'It would be, if I hadn't been ringside,' I muttered.

Carter looked down at the T-shirt draped across his knees. 'This is the first present she's ever bought me. Ever.'

Still nervous about being in the sitting room of an emotionally overwrought, six-foot trannie, I pulled out my phone. Still no message from Jordan. What was taking him so long?

'O'Loughlin know you're here?' Carter mumbled, looking up again, his big, blue eyes troubled. 'The day Mon arrived, she was a mess. Bruises all over. Cuts on her hands and face. Said O'Loughlin had found out she was seeing some younger, richer, more powerful dirt bag who'd promised to set her up, get her away from him for good. She said she was leaving him and it sent O'Loughlin into a frenzy—swore he'd shoot everyone starting with her and the dirt bag. But he started firing on strangers instead, didn't he? And in the mess and the screaming, she just crawled out from under and ran. Mon arrived on my doorstep dressed in some stranger's suit jacket. And a pair of sequinned hot pants with thigh high, white patent boots.'

His laughter sounded strangled as he waved his hand at the window.

'Mon even had the presence of mind to make the taxi driver drop her one block down on Clerkenwell Street. So no one would connect her to me. It was only luck the nosy neighbours were all at work—it was still peak hour then— and no one saw a bloody, half-naked woman knocking on my front door.'

I met Carter's gaze without flinching as I described to him the moment I'd stood on the train tracks inside Eve's dead memory and witnessed her fear.

'She'd been running from someone that night,' I murmured.

Carter went pale. 'Do you think it was him? O'Loughlin?'

He shivered, rubbing his bare arms and reaching for a packet of smokes and a lighter on a side table before pulling his hand back when he saw me looking.

'I don't have any answers, remember? Only questions,' I said, jumping as the sound of arguing voices erupted somewhere at the back of the house. Carter went white as the volume climbed and I finally worked out from the *hee haw, hee haw* of the laughter, the back and forth, that it was drive-time radio. A couple of comedians, going at it.

Then a silence, just as abrupt.

'You see?' Carter hunched over like he was in pain. 'Now the lights,' he murmured, almost absent-mindedly, as the single pendant light in the hallway went on and off, twice, the rhythm crisp and defined like a kid was playing with the switch.

I was hunching now, too, as I stared up at the three-armed chandelier in the ceiling, wondering if it was going to go next.

But she was feeling playful. Carter and I almost fell

off our seats as the sewing machine behind us sewed a phantom seam for a full ten seconds or more, then fell still and silent.

I found that I was hugging myself so tightly that it hurt.

'The first week after she disappeared,' Carter whispered through his fingers, 'the lights would flicker, or the radio would go, the TV. I'd be asleep and then *bam*. Beethoven. Or bible bashers. Ninja steak knives. Just enough to wake me. Just one thing. Not every night. A reminder, maybe. That she was still around.' He uncovered his face. 'As if I'd ever forget. But I tried to ignore it. It's not much, but this is my *house*. It's all I've got. She knows that. Knew. So I refused to look or engage or believe. Until last night.'

He rubbed at the stubble beneath his jawline with a rasping sound.

'I was asleep. I'd done two shows back-to-back. I was exhausted. Even the sound of a TV firing up on its own wouldn't have woken me and she knew it. So what does she do?'

I rocked forward, not wanting to hear, my crossed arms resting across the tops of my thighs.

'She *gets into bed with me*,' he murmured. 'The way she sometimes did when sleep wouldn't come and she wanted to talk, even if I didn't. It's her arms I'm feeling around my waist, her legs sliding through mine, her hair...' Carter's eyes were wild. 'It's lying across my pillow, I swear I can feel it, and I almost run out into the street, screaming. I actually beg her to show me how I'm supposed to help her. I'm screaming: *What am I supposed to do?*'

We both leap about a foot into the air as loud warning bells begin to clang outside.

Outside.

At the railway crossing.

Daughtry.

I was so relieved by the sound of the bells, I felt dizzy. Jordan would be here soon.

Without looking at me, Carter suddenly jumped to his feet and snatched up his smokes and lighter, stuffing them into a back pocket of his jeans. He grabbed a hair band out of a mess of clips in a tarnished silver bowl on a hallstand by the door and pulled his huge man-fro into a low bun. It made him look like a sixteen-year-old girl. A very scared, tall, flat-chested sixteen-year-old girl with the most beautiful eyes you'd ever see.

'Uh...' I said, as I half rose from my sagging armchair and glanced out the front window. *Any minute now, any minute, Jordan, Daughtry, please.*

Carter ignored me, shrugging hurriedly into a black hooded parka that had been hanging on a hook behind the sitting room door. He stuffed his long feet into a pair of flashy blue and yellow trainers, and the T-shirt from Eve into one of the large outer pockets of his coat.

Then, without waiting, Carter walked straight out his front door, slamming it behind him while the bells clanged and clanged incessantly.

What was *I* supposed to do now?

Cursing and calling, 'Wait! *Wait!*', I thumbed my phone on and sent Jordan a frantic text:

On the move. Come find me. Hurry.

16

I trailed Carter as he strode down Branxholme Street, his arms wrapped around his middle, head bowed. He didn't look back once. I still had my phone in my hand, waiting for a message from Jordan that wouldn't come. Carter was moving so quickly that we soon turned a corner and his house and the railway station were lost to sight.

Carter took a steady downhill path. As we crossed over street after street—the occasional lonely hoot of a train's siren sounding in the distance—we didn't encounter a single car or pedestrian.

A dog barked as we crossed a narrow stretch of tarred road lined with old timber houses and then I heard running water. We were in the cool green region of the map Jordan and I had pulled up on my computer at home.

A gloomy tangle of willow trees and prickly pear, and green things I didn't recognise, choked and twined beside a fast-flowing body of water. Every inch of me tingled in recognition.

Merri Creek.

It seemed more like a swollen river, the way it rushed and tumbled through the corridor of trees and low-hanging boughs. Soon, any evidence of human habitation was lost to sight. We were alone beside the racing water, enclosed in a dark canopy of green.

'Carter!' I called, suddenly craving the nearness of another living body. 'Wait up!'

He didn't, but slowed down enough for me to almost catch him as he crossed a narrow wooden foot bridge choked with plastic bottles, a sea of them bobbing against the footings, white as bones. Inexplicably, there was a large, silver TV sticking out of the centre of the fast flowing current, its partially snapped-off antennae doing a lopsided victory sign.

I crossed the slick wooden walkway to the opposite bank. The recent rains had been heavy, and the choked and swirling water came almost all the way up to the slats.

Carter's gait was purposeful. I kept pace behind him up the narrow bike trail. From the bank, I saw a mattress, an armchair, another TV, abandoned in the middle of the flow.

The temperature seemed to be lowering, the wind rising. If it weren't for the asphalt beneath my feet, the hard rubbish in the water, we might have entered a primeval time.

We passed lush banks of dandelion, nettles and blackberries gone wild with the rain. Turning another corner, whole bends of the creek—root and branch—were draped with shreds and streamers of ghostly bleached plastic that rippled in the wind; the harvest of a multitude of storm water drains. The sight was both eerie and beautiful.

The path hugging the creek gradually began climbing. I counted two more drowned TVs far out in the water, each one bigger than the last, analogue victims of the digital era. The second of these—the size of a small car—was buried at the foot of a huge, Victorian-era bluestone bridge, just outside the shadow of the giant arch. Carter and I passed beneath the bridge, and every footstep we took now echoed sharply. It seemed colder here, and I hurried to get through and out into what light remained.

The path ran steeply upwards after the bridge, spilling into a grassy nature reserve bordered by playing fields. The trees thinned out, and through the towering pines and gum trees, I saw that the sky was dark and leaden now, almost a night-time sky, though my phone told me it was just after 4pm.

Ahead, Carter was standing beside a drinking fountain, lighting the cigarette a man was holding out to him.

The stranger was stocky, with a broad, tanned face under a salt-and-pepper crew cut. He had on a shirt and blue jeans, and the kind of beat-up leather jacket Jordan would wear. Carter and I had inches on him, and I slowed as I got closer to them, unsure whether they knew each other and I was intruding.

The older guy spotted me hanging back on the footpath. 'Mind if I smoke?' he rasped. 'Dying for a smoke.'

Carter shook his head and lit his own cigarette, continuing to ignore me. While the older man looked at each of us in turn, Carter finished his first, grinding it out beneath the toe of his shoe, and started on another.

'About to bucket down,' the stranger said, gazing at the sky. 'Taking your life in your own hands, son, heading down this path.'

He blew a long stream of smoke at us before grinding out his smoke with one Cuban heel. With a friendly wave, he strode out towards the row of period, pretty-as-gingerbread houses bordering the reserve.

When the man was out of earshot, Carter abruptly started talking like he couldn't stop—like something inside him had broken.

'She was high strung, you know? She was running scams, running guys, left, right and centre. But a great girl, really. Fearless. You felt invincible when you were with Mon. She was outrageous: bigger, bolder, bustier than

201

anyone. Into everything: tabletop, escort work, glamour shots, promotionals. She'd get her clothes off for the opening of an envelope if there was money in it. She's always been a night owl, couldn't get her out of bed before two in the afternoon, it drove me bananas, but she was magnetic, you know? You couldn't look away from her. Even without the ice, the speed, the crack, she always had tonnes of energy. A real powerhouse…'

His voice broke and trailed away as he nervously lit another ciggie. I found his rambling description of her hard to reconcile with the sober, black-clad, barefoot figure with the unbound black hair that haunted me like a snatch of music I couldn't name. Eve looked like an unsmiling nun with no shoes.

'I told her I didn't want none of that shit at my place— the drugs, the toughs—so I suppose that's what she was doing when she wasn't hiding out from Keith O'Loughlin; trying to use or score on the sly, meeting up with the man *du jour*. So it's my fault she went out there that night, mine…'

He pushed the heel of one trembling hand against his nose and closed his eyes.

Carter's voice was calmer when he said, 'You weren't far wrong when you said she seemed a bit evil. She's like a tornado—had a knack of sucking all the air and goodwill out of a place in seconds flat. When she was good she was very, very good and when she was bad? You just got the hell out of there and kept running.'

Carter gave me a tremulous smile, the raw wind buffeting us both as he fumbled the T-shirt Monica had left him out of a pocket of his parka.

'We're never going to know how it ended,' he said, as the rain began to fall. 'So we make our own end, and our own peace. Come on. Before the moisture plays *havoc* with our hair, girlfriend.'

As he finished speaking, I realised Eve was standing behind him. And when she turned, he turned, too, as if to follow, though it was clear he couldn't see her. Only me.

It seemed fitting that she was there.

I pulled my hood back up uselessly over my head as the three of us passed back across the reserve under the tall pines, through the rain.

And through everything that nature threw at us, Eve remained inviolate: stern, serene, untouched by the elements. Beautiful.

So like my mother that the sight of her was like the feeling of a fishbone caught in the soft tissues of my throat.

✦

'This will do!' Carter shouted and his voice bounced off the undercarriage of the giant stone arch, black in the rain. The T-shirt was still wrapped around one fist, wet through now. He looked half-drowned, the curls against his temples lying flat and stringy against his pale skin, thin black streamers washing down from his eyes into his dark stubble.

As we'd backtracked through the downpour, Eve had dissipated before me without warning. So it was just Carter and me now, marooned inside a vast waterfall. Beyond the arch of the bridge, the air sizzled with rain, a wall of grey either side of us that seemed almost solid.

'At least it's drier under here,' Carter said, his words coming back at us in sibilant, echoing waves. 'Good a place as any.'

I knew that he'd brought us here to say goodbye. And it no longer surprised me that I was here, with him—some guy I barely knew. None of this seemed remotely strange any more. I realised that Eve was as voiceless and helpless as I used to feel, a ghost on the sidelines just wanting someone to notice she was there. When she'd been alive, we would never have had the slightest thing in common. But dead, she and I shared the condition of being cut off from the ordinary flow of life, and I knew I didn't want to accept that any more. She'd shown me that.

She is You, Eve had told Claudia P. But the words could have been meant for me.

Her gift to me was Jordan, and I meant to grab the

lifeline he represented with every ounce of my strength. If the guy ever showed up.

I shivered as Carter bent and hefted up a chunk of fallen rock, wrapping the T-shirt tightly around it before hurling it into the water. He was half laughing, half crying, as the missile flew in an arc through the air, splashing into the water partway to the huge TV someone had drowned at the edge of the arch.

'You didn't even get my size right, darling,' he was sobbing. 'Typical! RIP, Monny, RIP.'

As he hugged himself, he scanned the apex of the overpass above us. 'You can go now, you can go, princess, it's all good,' he whispered.

I couldn't help a tear running down my cheek, wondering if this was all it took to set her free. In the end, her unfinished business had been so simple: to find the one person who'd given her shelter when she needed it most to say *thank you*.

My mobile rang. The sound of it, cleanly echoing, made Carter and me jump. I drew the thing out of my pocket and the screen flashed up the name: *Jordan Haig*.

Holding up my hand to Carter in apology, I exclaimed, 'Thank God, J. where have you *been*?'

The static of a bad line greeted me. 'Hello?' I shouted. 'Hello? We're at the bridge, the big stone one, on the Merri Creek trail. Jordan? *Jordan?*'

Still hearing nothing but hissing, I dropped the phone as the world exploded into colours all around me.

✦

I knew I wasn't dead because my ears were ringing, and through it I could also discern screaming. It couldn't be coming from me, because I couldn't get any air into my body. Someone had, at some point, punched me in the head, and now they had me in an excruciating headlock. My face and neck were then forced so hard into the ground that pain exploded in my nose, behind my eyeballs. I could feel gravel and broken glass against my cheek, grass in my mouth, earth.

'See *this* coming, Nostradamus?' someone laughed, and the pressure eased just enough to let me take a single gagging breath before rough hands rolled me over again.

I whooped, soil coating my tongue, as I heard sounds of struggle somewhere to my left. Carter's cries abruptly stopped.

'Got the queer?'

Somebody else grunted. 'Yep.'

The rain beat down as I tried hard to focus my eyes, make sense of what I was looking at. Crouched over me was a rain-drenched stranger with a dark ponytail, huge shoulders and a paunch wearing a tooled leather vest, jeans and weathered Cuban-heeled boots. They were riding boots, I sluggishly realised. Dad had had some, said they were the only thing would give a proper grip, rain or shine.

No guy wore Cuban heels these days, unless they didn't give two shits what people thought of them, and had the muscle to back it up. Men like my Dad who'd owned a pair until he died. Died with them on.

I furrowed my grazed brow, trying to think, setting off fresh waves of pain in my face.

Reavers. These men were Reavers.

'O'Loughlin?' I croaked, trying to reconcile the tall, scowling, overweight figure with the grainy photo I'd seen on the internet of the man still on the run. Could be. Give or take twenty kilograms and a dye job.

'O'Loughlin's not far,' someone laughed. The speaker was standing somewhere over the paunchy guy's shoulder, far enough back I couldn't see him. 'Coppers think he's reached Queensland by now,' the voice added. 'But we know better.'

There was a round of laughter as Ponytail forced my head around, hard. I found myself looking, through watering eyes, at the creek flowing by, around and past the big, black TV buried in the swell, my neck at an impossible angle. Any moment now, I was going to break.

'Still good for something, those TVs,' the speaker said conversationally. 'All the locals dump their unwanted shit here, so we followed suit.'

Horror engulfed me. 'What did you do to Eve?' I gagged, already knowing the answer.

'*Who?*' said Ponytail sharply, looking over his shoulder and shrugging in the direction of his unseen companions.

'Monica, I mean,' I coughed. 'Monica Cybo.'

'Now this is the problem in a nutshell,' snarled the man I couldn't see. 'Everybody here knows far too much for my liking.'

I knew I was going to die. Some part of me prayed I'd be back at school on Monday morning like none of this had ever happened; back learning the rules from the ground up—the nice girl who was good for a laugh, the chick who could take a joke, who was always a good sport but nobody's bestie—back to watching Jordan Haig from a distance and wondering what he was thinking, whether he ever even thought about me for a nanosecond. But I'm a realist, and even as my eyes continued to probe for a way out, I knew it was out of my hands and only blind luck would save me now.

As if to crush even that thought, the man I couldn't see said calmly, 'I did unto Mon what I did to Curtis Fallon, Bony Lincoln and a list of others too long to mention—killed them the same way I had someone take out your fucking woman-stealing prick of a father. Patience has its own rewards. Always get what you want, in the end.'

I began to tremble uncontrollably as the implacable voice added, 'The irony is you coulda been *my* kid if your slut of a mum hadn't run off with my right-hand man.'

I knew who he was. What had Mum said? No man ever left the Reavers, the brotherhood you took to your grave. Eve and the other woman, Nadja, were just replacements, look-alikes, warm bodies, for the one that got away from him years ago.

I began to moan—long and low like a dying animal— and the three men standing around me laughed and let me go on making that awful noise because it was the last sound I was ever going to make.

Until the temperature abruptly dropped, and all the noise in me was cut off.

Suddenly, the air was like broken glass, stabbing into my throat, my lungs. It hurt to breathe. The air on my skin, it all hurt.

Everyone felt it. I knew it by the way Ponytail shivered and whined, distracted, 'Boss, do we do it here? It's cold.'

The rain was almost deafening, but it wasn't the rain making the big man uneasy, it was the sudden and pervasive smell of violets. Like someone had just dropped and busted a big bottle of perfume, the smell rising all around us, staining everything.

My wildcard. My beautiful, vengeful siren.

Ponytail shook me. 'What's the idea?' he snarled. I

shook my head, pointing weakly over his shoulder and heard collective gasping.

It was like the first time I ever saw her.

Eve was silent and resolute, her entire body limned in a soft silver beneath the shadowy arch, looking as real as you or me. But this time, her focus was elsewhere. Her eyes were fixed on that big, black TV sticking up out of the water at a crazy angle, a good three-quarters submerged.

Ponytail scrambled away so quickly he fell over me with a crunch and kept right on scrambling.

'Boss?' the other man standing over Carter quavered. I could hear the creak and scuff of leather as he edged away, towards the curtain of rain on the far side of the bridge.

The man the others called *Boss* moved forward, and I saw that it was the smoker from the park. O'Loughlin looked nothing like his photo.

As O'Loughlin stared at Eve's advancing figure his eyes were almost bugging out of his pale, strained face, but his voice was all controlled venom. 'Once a bitch, always a bitch,' he breathed. 'I'll put you down again if I have to, you dog...'

I didn't catch what happened next because this was blind luck happening right here, and if I could get across the water to the path on the other side of the creek, there would be houses, people who could help me.

I rolled onto my stomach and slithered down the embankment towards the creek bed as O'Loughlin screamed at his men, *'Get her!'*

17

But Eve was repaying me in kind for all the things she'd made me do; all the loose ends I'd tied up on her behalf. I'd been faithful, I'd shown compassion, and now she brought the raw wind with her, the storm.

O'Loughlin, I thought I heard her shriek, the wind her voice. *O'Lough-liiiiiin*.

Spooked, I tumbled headlong down the rocky embankment. All I could hear was the sound of men screaming, and the rain.

I plunged into the icy water, gasping as it quickly rose above my knees. Half-blind in the darkness beneath the arch, I moved in the direction of the abandoned TV parting the current, intending to skirt around it. The walking track on the opposite bank terminated just beyond the TV. If I followed the path back, and cut through the scrub on that side, it wouldn't be long before I hit houses.

Behind me, I heard the thrash and roar of an angry man entering the water and I scrambled out of the shadow of the bridge into the grey open air. The rain struck me like bullets and my hair was soon plastered to my skull, run-off streaming straight into my eyes. I was so stiff, so cold, that only fear kept me going.

The water now rose up beyond my hips, then my waist, as I passed to the left of the TV, giving it a wide berth. Suddenly, pain struck through my right shoulder blade and I lost my footing and went down, flailing, drinking water.

I felt a big hand grip me by the back of the neck. I was dragged face-first through the swell. The fist yanked me upwards like baggage.

As I coughed and gagged for air, O'Loughlin snarled into the side of my face, 'What Monica failed to understand, is that your kind are *made to be thrown away*. You, Mon, Joss, Angel—only exist because we *permit* it.'

He pushed me under again, dragging me beneath the surface of the murky water until my face was inches away from the slime lying along the bottom of the creek.

I caught a glimpse of a bright-blue tarp buried in the silt, flattened beneath the edge of the abandoned TV.

O'Loughlin held me down, thrashing and foaming,

beginning to see rainbows, at the very limits of my endurance.

Suddenly, he pushed me face-first into the mud, like it was a taster of things to come, and I expelled what little air I had left in my lungs. The creek bed yielded, the mud clinging to every contour of my face, and my frantic movements only exposed more of the cylindrical, tarpaulin-wrapped thing jammed into the filth. I cried out, as I realised what it was, dirt and rot and water streaming into my mouth, drinking it in.

It was *what remained*. What Eve had really wanted Jordan and me to find.

O'Loughlin abruptly let go, and I clawed my way to the surface, spitting and hacking, lashing out at him, even though I was blind.

He cuffed me in the face and I fell, the back of my head slamming into the edge of the TV screen. The world threatened to go black. O'Loughlin knotted one of his fists into the thick fabric around my waist to keep me from sliding further into the water, while his other hand disturbed the depths around us, looking for something.

'Mon's trouble was that she overestimated her importance,' he shouted through the beating rain. 'She *demanded* I choose, and when I wouldn't, she started offering herself around.'

I could hear his disbelief.

'No one leaves *me*. No one.' He bent lower in the water, grunting. 'She brought it all on *herself*. Just as your Dad did, and Angel.'

O'Loughlin squatted suddenly, yanking something out of the murk, his face red and straining with effort. In his hand was a rusty spade, encrusted with mud from the creek bed.

He hooked the handle of the spade over one of the broken TV antennae and turned me roughly so my face was pressed into the top of the set. He pulled my head back by the hair, wedging my body tight against the screen with the weight of his own body. I felt his hips grind into me from behind and felt a visceral fear.

'Like that, do you? Your mum did.'

His laughter was hateful and I caught the silver glisten of a knife blade from the corner of one straining eye, my throat curved back, taut and exposed. The spade, hooked alongside me, stank.

'The rain will wash it all away,' he said kindly. 'And you'll be mud. Just like all of them.'

There was a roaring darkness inside my head as I waited for the final blow, too weak to do more than hang there in his grip, drawing one rasping breath after another.

I was on the verge of closing my eyes, when there was a shiver in the air. Before me, the grey twilight, the rain, seemed to tease apart.

Just the faintest gap in reality, unfurling so quickly—along the vertical, then the horizontal—that a field of waving grass flashed into existence, rising in the distance into gentle, undulating hills. Wildflowers blanketed the green-gold grass to the horizon, and the sky was violet, rainless, filled with scudding white clouds.

A vision, maybe. My last.

'So beautiful,' I murmured aloud, greedy for that place, that peace, and O'Loughlin shook me. 'Whaddaya on about?' he grunted.

I struggled fitfully, wanting O'Loughlin's attention fixed solely on me. It was no place for someone like him. I didn't want him to see it. He didn't deserve that.

I kicked out, suddenly, and he was caught by surprise. I slid down lower, into the water. O'Loughlin was forced to bend and haul me up, grunting. It would even be okay—this stupid, unpoetic ending, I told myself—if I could just wake *there*, walk beneath that violet sky.

The breach was so close now. Just a surge through the water, and I'd be there. I'd be through.

It might as well have been miles. O'Loughlin re-positioned me belly-down against the TV, digging the knife tip into the left side of my throat as he hissed into my ear, 'Say hello to Joss and Angel for me.'

Two skies, one inside the other. Maybe they'd be waiting, Joss and Angel, just over the rise.

Take me there, I begged silently.

As if my words had called them to me, over a distant hill inside that impossible hallucination, two figures came running. Tiny as insects.

I frowned, trying to make them out, as O'Loughlin pulled my head back by the hair.

At the sight of me, the two runners seemed to pick up speed, the one in the lead raising his hand and giving a ringing, warning shout that echoed down the mystical valley before me, causing even O'Loughlin to raise his head and *look*.

Straight into the gap.

Mouth gaping, he rasped, '*What*—' His hold on me slackened in surprise.

The fracture was now wide enough, real enough, to step through. Grasping one of the TV's antennae for support, I began inching away from O'Loughlin around the side of the drowned machine.

My lips were moving with effort, though no sound came. I knew for a fact that if I could make it to the gap, O'Loughlin would never be able to touch me again.

But O'Loughlin knew it, too. 'No you don't,' he grunted behind me. Pain exploded again in my back as he stabbed down.

I screamed, my hold on the antenna loosening.

O'Loughlin stabbed me again, twisting the blade. And

I knew that the two men in the distant valley caught my scream of agony. Knew that it echoed over the waving green-gold field and hung beneath that violet sky.

Two figures, running, the last thing I might ever see: the one in the lead fluid as water, long-limbed, broad-shouldered, his long, blond hair streaming out behind him as he leapt through the hip-high grass; Jordan's rangy, familiar, beloved shape so close behind.

I sobbed, sinking lower beneath the current as O'Loughlin stuck me one last time for certainty, for luck, cursing as his blade became entangled in the fabric of my hood. He had to push my body off the blade, shoving me aside so carelessly that the antenna I was gripping onto snapped off in my hand.

Then he moved past me, towards the widening breach, knife out before him, as I sank beneath the surface.

I could taste my iron blood in the water, seeping out. Regretted that I would never get to walk beneath that sky, with Joss, with Angel, with Jordan.

So easy, just to surrender.

But then something lit in me, like flame, like the north wind.

O'Loughlin, I heard myself roar through the tumbling water, the wind my voice.

O'Lough-liiiiiin.

I was on my feet when I shouldn't have been able to

stand; blood and water streaming off my body, monstrous. And *she* was in me, gripping tight like claws hooked around my soul, the effort to stay, to speak, so terrible.

She cried out through my lips, through my throat, in a voice that was not my voice, deep, husky, laughing, '*Sheol*, O'Loughlin. I've been waiting to take you there, my love. We each get the ever after we deserve, you'll see.'

O'Loughlin stilled in shock, turning. Framed between me and the fracture in reality that every part of my soul, and hers, longed for.

Giving a high, animal scream of rage, he charged at me through the water with his hunting knife raised high.

Through me, I felt Eve stretch. And it felt to me, for a moment, as if I possessed the hard muscles and strength of a dancer. But then I bent double, retching, curving my arms around my body, almost dropping the broken antenna still clutched in my right hand, as Eve relived some unimaginable pain. Her unimaginable hold on me wavering.

'Die, you bitch,' O'Loughlin breathed over me, the rain pouring down like it would never stop. 'Just *die*.'

Then the knife came at me again, and Eve and I curled ourselves one into the other, drawing strength, pulling tight, so that before the blade could touch me, I twisted and swung upwards with the thin, broken piece of antenna in my hand and buried it in the soft flesh of his throat.

Blood pouring. Rivers of it, from him, from me.

We fell away from each other, O'Loughlin and me.

Then I felt Eve lift through me and out, before the water claimed me.

18

I fell into the water and imagined I saw the sky.

It was violet. Clouds passed overhead, moving fast. There was no rain, no sound.

Then, without warning, I was pulled out of the water, and the sound of the driving rain resumed. I could feel the whole world tilting as Jordan carried me beneath a canopy of dark green.

He sank to his knees on the bike path I'd been so desperate to reach before, laying me down in the shadow of a massive willow whose branches swept overhead before trailing into the water. I lay against the wall of his chest in a cathedral of green, breathing shallowly. It hurt to do more.

'Daughtry, goddamn you,' Jordan screamed. 'Where *are* you? Daughtry! Help me. *Please.*'

I couldn't seem to hold my head up and it slipped to one side so that I saw it, the gap, just for a moment. The one that Jordan and Daughtry must have run through to reach me because Daughtry half turned then in the water. One foot already inside the fracture between two worlds. As he stepped back, the fracture closed and I could have imagined everything. There was only the drowned TV, the current, O'Loughlin floating facedown, in the water.

Daughtry was tall, with thick blond hair worn unfashionably long and wind-tangled, I realised, from running. As I watched, he plaited the golden mass of it swiftly and bound the end of it. And then I knew who he was. I had last seen him, standing over my bed, when I was a very small child. I had no energy left to question, only wonder.

He hadn't changed, in all the intervening years. I could see he was wearing the same plaid shirt pulled tight across hard shoulders, dark, narrow jeans plastered to his legs by the current. As he came out of the water towards us, I saw that he was wearing old-fashioned, lace-up leather ankle boots that looked like they'd been hacked out of the cured hide of some furry animal. Like Jordan, he appeared to have a couple of kilograms of silver and onyx fastened around his wrists and neck.

His dark green eyes regarded me with an almost tender

amusement as he climbed up the embankment. I couldn't look away as Daughtry threaded the dark, spindle-shaped stick of wood he was holding—a sharp, doubled-ended thing, the length of one hand from wrist to fingertips—through the base of his plait.

'When you expect him he doesn't show,' I murmured, 'and when you don't, he just materialises out of nowhere.'

It made sense now. Daughtry could take shortcuts others could only dream of. I could see confirmation of this in Jordan's dazed expression. I began to cough, my mouth filling up with blood as Daughtry knelt and took my hand.

Jordan dialled, speaking in clipped frantic tones as I whispered, rain and blood mingling in my mouth, 'Am I going to die?'

I closed my eyes and could still see: *Two skies, one inside the other.*

And a valley filled with wildflowers of every colour, dotted across green-gold grass. The lavender farm of my dream. If I could get there, keep walking, maybe I would find him, Dad, and he would take me to Mum, and my heart squeezed tight at the thought. It was so close, I could almost touch it. It was just beyond that gap.

'Make it come back,' I gargled, stirring fitfully as Jordan tried to hold me still while he pleaded with someone on the line. 'Take me with you.'

Daughtry said in his smoky voice, 'Not yet. Not for you. Though I told you you were intriguing, Sophie, and you are.'

He took my hand and I could feel the scars and calluses there. The hand of a man who wielded heavy things, who knew how to fight. In a formal voice, I heard him say something like: *Jorn der Ort Reeve*.

Frowning with my eyes closed, I blurted before I could think, 'That's not a name. I can't even spell that.'

'Then I shall spell it for you,' he laughed, saying with exaggerated courtesy, 'J-e-a-n d-e H-a-u-t R-i-v-e. It is both a name, and a place name. It is where I am from: *Haut Rive*. It means, *the high bank*, or something of that kind.'

I opened my eyes with difficulty, unable to reply for the coughing.

Daughtry gestured at the landscape around us, the creek below, and his voice and gaze were suddenly urgent.

'I want you to stay here. Don't go to that place, Sophie, do you understand? *Don't go looking for anyone you know.* Just wait. Here, with Jordan. You're one of us now, whether you like it or not. You are *mastin*; a gate keeper. But wholly unprepared, untrained. Can you do that? Wait here?'

He had to lean close to hear me murmur, 'Where did she go? Eve?'

Daughtry took both my hands in his and his green eyes seemed to glow for a moment.

'*Sheol*, Sophie, where freed souls reside. There are

things I must do there—the newly dead are very powerful. They have not yet forgotten what it means to be alive. Do not leave Jordan until I come for you both. You're safe here. I will try to be as quick as I can. But you must hold on.'

He rose, looking down at me as Jordan repeated his directions with wild eyes. 'Just wait, Sophie. It won't be long.'

Daughtry inclined his head and stepped back, sliding the spindle-shaped piece of wood back out of his knotted hair. He turned with a rapid motion and re-entered the water, slashing a quick vertical line, then a horizontal one, in the air behind him, before spinning back to face me.

The air behind him began to separate.

An indistinct piece of nothing seemed to grow and unfurl behind Daughtry's back until I caught a shift in shape and colour and light that jarred with the rain lashed landscape I lay in.

Daughtry held my gaze steadily for a moment more, calling, 'Stay with Jordan, Sophie. Or risk being lost inside Sheol forever.'

Then he was gone, and the breach with him, and my entire world was Jordan's rain-drenched face over mine.

He threw his phone aside and wrapped me tightly in his arms, pleading, 'You don't go anywhere without me, you hear?'

But my eyes were already closing, and the smell of wildflowers, the feel of sunshine, were growing stronger.

Acknowledgments

With thanks to my loving husband, Michael, and our beautiful children, Oscar, Leni and Yve; who put up with much, and light my way in this world.

With thanks also to Yean Kai and Susan Lim, Ruth and Eugenia Lim, Barry and Judy Liu, Ben and Michelle Lee and Sally and Marcus Price, for all that they do for me throughout the writing year.

With enormous thanks also to my publisher, Michael Heyward, and my editor, Rebecca Starford, and all at The Text Publishing Company in Melbourne (best city in the world!) including, but not limited to, the wonderful Alice Cottrell, Hannah Forrest, Anne Beilby, Kirsty Wilson, Emily Booth, Alice Lewinsky, Imogen Stubbs,

Stephanie Speight and Shalini Kunahlan. And to Alison Arnold—who welcomed me into the charmed circle in the first place—with thanks and best wishes always.

This is a work of fiction. All of the names, characters, descriptions and events in this book are entirely fictional, and all opinions expressed by the characters are expressed by the characters; whose preferences and attitudes are also entirely their own. Any errors are entirely mine.

Certain authorial liberties may have been taken with those buildings and places that do actually exist in the real world and, for those, the author apologises and begs your leave.